"Cora Schwartz has written a provocative novel of unforgettable faces and locales that will deeply move even the most diehard cynic. She lures her compelling characters to crawl under the reader's skin and settle in for a long winter's nap. I will be remembering Rudy for a long time to come."

Linda Bergman
Bergman Entertainment, "So You Think Your Life's a Movie"

"A remarkable love story set in the aftermath of the Holocaust. Cora Schwartz has captured the strain of living with a survivor and trying to grasp the unfathomable. It's a film waiting to happen."

Francine Silverman
Radio host of "Book Marketing with Fran"

"As someone who has written a memoir in novel form, I am well aware of the difficulty of this task: remaining true to the central remembered events yet writing with the flow of a novel that will interest a reader. In the case of Cora Schwartz this difficulty is many times multiplied by the unfamiliar setting that she had to make real and by the depiction of her mate, who was not only a survivor of the Holocaust, with all that that entailed, but someone who had fallen under the spell of the gypsies (hence the title) and incorporated some of their (to us) totally alien ways. Cora Schwarz has done a magnificent job of surmounting all these difficulties and giving us a memoir/novel that is highly significant in itself yet engrossing and fascinating. As the book goes on, I found that it became more and more compelling and so will any reader who comes to it with a mind open to the unfamiliar—but alive with vibrant humanity, as Cora and her story richly are. I recommend it in the highest terms. Do read it. It will be a powerful experience and at the same time a great treat!"

Dr. Maurice Friedman
Professor Emeritus of Religious Studies, Philosophy and Comparative Literature at San Diego State University. Author of Abraham Joshua Heschel and Elie Wiesel: You Are My Witnesses

"A moving and spirited story of love and loss, told with passion and a commitment to heal the world."

Marianne Hirsch
Professor of English and Comparative Literature
Institute for Research on Women and Gender
Columbia University

"This racy tale of love, sex, and cross-cultural mysteries is reminiscent of the enigmatic relationships in Goethe's 1809 novel *Elective Affinities*. Autobiography and biography are mixed in often luridly gripping encounters between our Bronx-raised Jewish author and her Ukraine-raised Jewish lover, the hard-drinking, gambling, erratic but strangely steady, Nazi camp survivor, Rudy.

(Over:)

Their 'elective affinity' for each other, against all the odds of differences in background and outlook, has a familiar ring. For me it recalls the 'wish and will to belong' that I found to make for the needed cement, mutual trust, between adoptive parents and children. Even without Ms. Schwartz's breathless storytelling, her *Gypsy Tears* would be a cliff-hanger."

H. David Kirk
Professor Emeritus, University of Waterloo, and Adjunct Professor, University of Victoria, Author of Shared Fate *and* Adoptive Kinship

"We loved it! From the first paragraph, there was something very inviting, like an old friend or familiar voice, like a scene from Casablanca that you can hear in the background and see in your mind's eye, and perhaps even pretend to be a part of. Even with a house full of people around the holidays, we actually could not put it down, and its been a very long time since we could make such a claim."

Shirley & Giora Gerzon
Producer and Director of award winning "The Olympic Doll"

"A passionate love story, *Gypsy Tears* reminds us that deep attachment has a mysterious and unknowable side that transcends conventional thinking. Cora Schwartz has written an inspiring story of profound committment despite her beloved's all-too-human foibles."

Susan Richards
Marriage and Family Therapist, L.C.S.W. / M.F.T.

"I'm a Holocaust survivor, and in my childhood in 1941–1944 I went through what Rudy did. I remember everything that the Nazis did with the Jews and the Gypsies, and when I read the book, tears filled my eyes.

We have to remember it and never forget it. We have to tell it to other people and let them know how it was. This book by Cora Schwartz is a work of fiction, but it is based on real facts. That is why I confirm that it is a very useful book, and people have to read it."

Yakov Goldfedib
Holocaust survivor

"A haunting and ultimately heartbreaking love story which reveals the continuing lethal effects of the Holocaust on its survivors and those who love them. Readers will be swept off their feet by Rudy's fatal charm and will be left feeling pity and fear at the end of this tragic and beautiful novel. A must-read for anyone interested in the destructive force of survivor guilt and the mysterious healing powers of the human heart."

Dr. Rhoda Sirlin
Professor of English at Queens College, CUNY. Author of Crime & Self-Punishment *and* Sophie's Choice: A Contemporary Casebook

Gypsy Tears

Loving a Holocaust Survivor

Cora Schwartz

HOBBLEBUSH BOOKS
Brookline, New Hampshire

Composed in Janson Text at
Hobblebush Books, Brookline, New Hampshire

Printed in the United States of America

10 9 8 7 6 5 4 3 2 1

This book is a work of fiction and, though it is based on a true story, the characters and events are fictional.

Publisher's Cataloging-In-Publication Data
(Prepared by The Donohue Group, Inc.)

Schwartz, Cora T.
  Gypsy tears : loving a Holocaust survivor / Cora Schwartz.

  p. ; cm.

  ISBN: 978-0-9760896-9-8

  1. Holocaust survivors—Fiction. 2. Holocaust, Jewish (1939-1945)—Ukraine—Fiction. 3. Romanies—Ukraine—Fiction. 4. Jewish women—United States—Fiction. 5. Ukraine—Fiction. 6. Historical fiction. I. Title.

  PS3619.C49 Gy 2007
  813/.6
2007923022

Published by:
Hobblebush Books

17-A OLD MILFORD ROAD
BROOKLINE, NEW HAMPSHIRE 03033

www.hobblebush.com

to Rudy,
who would have loved to see this book

Acknowledgments

Thank you to Louise Albert, who never stopped believing in me; Pat Carr and Stephanie Kaplan Cohen, who never stopped believing in this story; and Zoya Danilovich, who never stopped believing in Rudy.

CHAPTER 1

Rudy insisted on calling our rented basement apartment his bunker even though I complained it was depressing me. Except for the little, ground-level window over our bed, we were cut off from the outside world. He said that was what he liked the most, that and the hard cotton mattress propped up on cinder blocks in the corner. I cannot remember how he convinced me to rent the dismal place, but I do remember the first night the nightmares came. The tortured sounds he made were like the escalating howl of a wolf.

"Tell me." I shook him with trembling hands. "Tell me what you just dreamed."

Rudy mumbled, "I don't remember" and rolled over.

"You must remember. It just happened."

"Please, I don't remember. Just let me go back to sleep."

"Don't you dare turn your back on me. You just woke me out of a deep sleep. I want to know."

"There is nothing to know. Believe me."

"Why do you say that? You think because I can't see your face I don't know you're lying."

Rudy groaned and went back to sleep.

Most nights, the resentment of being jolted out of my sleep, with my heart pounding in my ears, kept me awake for hours.

I'd crawl out of our bed, fix a cup of tea on the hot plate, and watch the morning light slip under the curtain and settle on the top of his head. I did not struggle all that much, any more than I struggled with his other eccentricities. I knew Rudy needed to be down there, and for some reason I did too.

On those nights, I thought a lot about our first meeting that day in the Catskills. I was visiting my mother at the Shady Nook Senior Citizen Hotel when the handsome stranger in the black bathing suit walked up to me. He gestured with his head toward the men behind him. "But *you* know there is a Romania, don't you? Tell them there is a Romania."

"But of course!" I raised my voice so they could hear. "Everyone knows there's a Romania."

"Thank you." The stranger winked at me. "They didn't believe me."

"Oh." I brought my finger to my lips and leaned over. He bent down to meet me. I realized by the wrinkles at the corners of his eyes and the wisps of gray hair around his temples that he was older than I thought.

"Actually," I whispered, "I don't know that I do either. Isn't Romania just a song?"

"Well, then," he whispered back, "I'll take you there. I'll take you home." He lowered my hand to the table. "We will find the best gypsy music. You can help me find the ring! Would you like that?"

I stared at him. "The ring?"

"Yes, of course. This is the moment that could change every-thing. It was meant to be." He raised one eyebrow and waited.

I remember thinking he was just another crazy man. I was thirty-two years old and divorced. God knows I'd met plenty of crazies. I glanced at the book in my lap and considered moving my chair, but instead I looked up and smiled. "Thank you. I'd like that."

"Good. Meet me tonight. We can plan our trip."

He walked back to the men in a slow, deliberate way with hips that seemed to rotate effortlessly. He placed one long foot before the other as though he had invented walking. He stopped and lit a cigarette, resting his weight on one leg, bending the other at the knee. I wondered if he knew I was studying him. I was fascinated with the delicate manner with which his fingers held the cigarette, the way he threw his head back with narrowed eyes to avoid the smoke, dragging as though anxious to get it over with. That he wasn't an American seemed to be in the air around him. His brief bathing suit certainly looked European. I imagined his touch and how his leg would feel against mine.

He talked with the other men for a minute, placed his lit cigarette in an ashtray, and walked toward the pool. It was a blistering afternoon. He splashed around with some youngsters at the shallow end, then waded deeper where the water was up to his chest. His arms were up close to his body. He looked scared, like he was holding his breath. In another minute he was out.

"Afraid of the water?" I called out.

"I'm just not what you call a swimmer." His body was golden in the light. He smiled and the sun glinted off his white teeth.

He moved back to his chair in that same deliberate way,

collected his things, and walked across the hotel lawn without looking back. The strange melody he whistled trailed behind him.

My mother came up behind me. She swatted me lightly on the shoulder. "You see, I told you."

"Told me what, Mama?"

"I told you to come up here and visit me. Look, look at that nice man you were talking to. I told you."

"Yes, Mama, he does seem nice, doesn't he? But he is a little old."

"Old, shmold. He's handsome, that's all that counts. So, did he ask you for your number in the city? Did he?"

"Mama, it doesn't work that way."

"Sure it does. You have to show a little interest, that's all. Just show a little interest for God's sake."

"Mama, please, why don't you understand? I'm not interested."

"There's no such thing. Look at you. You're still young. You need more makeup. That's what it is."

My mother started to wear makeup after my father died. Suddenly she looked like her mother, Grandma Bessie. It was strange too how easily I now called her Mama after all the years of not wanting to even call her Mother. I even tolerated her pestering me about how I was wasting my life without a man. I accepted that she was incapable of understanding what it was like to survive the kind of marriage I'd had and that now I was happy alone. But last night, her phone call from the Catskills hotel made me feel guilty. I tossed some clothes in my bag and drove up to Shady Nook.

Her friends plucked at me. They patted my hair, pinched my cheek, and called me a maidala, a girl. Mama had tears in her eyes. They were all watching me from their benches under the trees when the Romanian stranger walked over to me.

"Maybe you want to know why he's here with all these old farts," Mama added.

"Who?"

"That man. The one you just talked to. His name is Rudy. Maybe you want to know. Weren't you wondering what he is doing here?"

"Well, yes. At least he's younger than most of the people here."

"He came to see the owner, Mr. Hirsch. They were in the camps together."

"You mean concentration camps?"

"What else?"

"I never met anyone who's been in the camps."

"So now maybe you'll pay him a little attention?"

Rudy did most of the talking that night. The faint scent of wine on his breath pleased me as we walked down the country road. The sun played games from behind the mountain. He took my hand after only a few minutes, and when the evening air turned cool, and without asking, he took off his blazer and put it around me. I turned my head to smell the cologne on its shoulder. His stride was much longer than mine. I had to take two steps to his one.

I sat on a bench on a wooden bridge. He stood off to the side behind me looking out at the lake. He was in the middle of a sentence when a series of distant explosions cut through the silence. I turned in time to see him jump.

I laughed. "They're only firecrackers."

"Yes. I know. But they bring back memories."

"You used to set off firecrackers when you were a boy?"

Rudy lit another cigarette before answering. "I was never a boy."

"You have an accent. Where are you really from?"

"You have one too, but I know where you are from. The Bronx."

"And you?"

"Oh, here and there."

"Like where?"

"I come from nowhere. I have no country, no home. Nobody wants me. I'm a gypsy."

"What about Romania? Remember, you're taking me to Romania. Isn't that where you're from?"

Another firecracker went off. Rudy moved so close to me I couldn't help thinking he was frightened.

"So where were you in March 1944?" he asked. "Were you nice and safe in the Bronx with your mommy bringing you orange juice in the morning?"

"Huuh, well yes, you might say that. Yes. What about it? I was just a little girl then, you know. Why? Where were you?"

"I can tell you I wasn't in a bed." Rudy sat down next to me. "My mommy wasn't bringing me orange juice either. I can tell you that much. I was busy surviving."

"Why are you so angry?" I pretended to fix my skirt as I put more space between us. "We all struggle to survive."

"You're sure about that?" Rudy looked at me. "Are you sure?"

"Sure I'm sure."

"Well, imagine this." He grabbed my hand and pulled me to the railing. He pointed out over the lake. "Imagine that a boy has to swim across that water down there. The moon is out just like this. Only it is March. He is swimming to meet an older boy from the other side. The older boy is bringing him a can of salt. Salt. Only it's not a lake."

Rudy's hand tightened around mine. "It's a river with a current. The boy is a good swimmer with strong legs. The typhus in the camp burned up his brain so he is not afraid. He will do anything for the salt. They need it. He gets to the middle and treads water. He waits. The older boy appears out of the darkness only two meters away, the can of salt tied to his back. The boy exchanges his gold for the can. Neither boy says a word. The older boy smiles and nods. Each boy takes a few strokes and waves goodbye as the spotlights go on. The younger boy turns and starts swimming as fast as he can. The bullets hit the water with little splashes. In the darkness behind him there is a cry."

Rudy let go of my hand and gripped the railing.

"'Do not think,' the boy says to himself with each stroke. 'Do not think.' He hears the guards shouting. He hears their motors whining. They are coming after him."

Rudy seemed to have told the story in one breath.

"What a story." I was breathless as well.

His flat voice filled the air around us. "It's not a story."

"Oh, I'm sorry." I wiped away my tears.

"Yes I know. Everybody was sorry. They all cried gypsy tears. Eight million people died anyway."

"Eight million? I thought it was six million."

"Six million Jews. Two million gypsies."

"What about the gypsy tears?"

"Real tears are dry tears, inside where you can't see them. You see there is survival and there is survival."

"I understand. I'm a bit of a survivor myself. It's just that I never heard a story like that, never knew anyone who lived through that. I really am sorry."

"Yes I know."

Rudy led me back to the bench. He stretched his arm along the back of it, crossed his legs, and took my hand. He turned it over and studied it the way Grandma Bessie used to do when she was pretending to read my palm. He rubbed his thumb across my life line. "I know you are sorry." His voice was suddenly gentle. "And I know you."

"But we met only three hours ago."

"Oh, but I have always known you. You can feel it. Don't you feel it?"

I contemplated his profile in the moonlight, his broad forehead, his fine nose, and the straight, tight line of his mouth. The air was still except for the chirping sounds of crickets. I took a deep breath.

My serious voice surprised me. "Yes, I do."

"Good." Rudy brought my hand to his lips and kissed it. He turned it over and kissed the palm. "Shall we?"

I didn't know what to say. "But it's so dark."

"It doesn't matter. I can see in the dark. But that's another long story." Rudy stood up and pulled me with him.

"Oh, you have to tell me."

"Someday." Rudy was laughing again. "Someday I'll tell you everything. But you have to promise one thing. You will have to believe me. You will have to believe everything."

Most nights I came home late from work and found Rudy rolled up in the colorful covers and spreads he brought back from his Eastern European trips. Gypsy violins cried on the record player. The disconnected phone plug hung from the wall. The wine bottle was almost always empty.

One night, as usual, I tiptoed to the corner and stooped down into the darkness. "Rudy?" I whispered. I held my breath, wondering if he was alive. He usually didn't respond right away, which scared me even more. Gradually he stirred, groped for my hand, brought it to his lips and kissed it.

"Schveetheart," he said, trying once again to sound like

Humphrey Bogart. "You've come back to me." His hushed voice reached deep inside me. It was always the same, the reaching out, the pressure of his kiss on my hand, the relief in his voice. "You've come back to me."

"Where else would I find a warm bed this time of night?" I used my most sarcastic voice, hoping he didn't know the truth.

Rudy pressed my cold palm between his warm cheek and his pillow.

"Do you mind if I at least take off my coat?" I tried to stand. He hung on for a second but then let go.

"Look at you," I said as I walked around the room, pulling off my skirt and blouse. "Look at this place, a damn gypsy tent. I can't live like this."

His muffled voice came out from the darkness. "You love it."

He was right. Faded, curled pictures of his people back in Chernovtsy were tacked on the wall over our bed. I knew that the pillows thrown in the corners and the damask throws piled over our few pieces of furniture took him far away to the place he called home.

Later that night, after yet another one of his nightmares, I studied the sink filled with unwashed wine glasses and watched again as the early morning light spread over his forehead.

Some nights Rudy yelled out more from having had too much wine than anything else. Half asleep, half in a drunken stupor, he answered my questions as though watching himself on a screen.

"Thirteen, voices in a cemetery. Can't run," he'd moan. "My feet, frozen."

"Where are you?" I'd whisper.

"Mogelov. Walking, frozen, numb."

"Where are you going?"

"Home. Mamala, the blanket. Rudichka always comes back."

"Who's with you."

"Mama Eva, bread."

When there were tears on Rudy's cheeks, I stopped and waited until the next time.

Rudy could also be a sober storyteller, most times telling the same story over and over. I always listened as though it was the first time because I knew that's what he needed. Right before our first trip to Chernovtsy, where he was born, Rudy started to tell his stories all over again. It was obvious he wanted to impress me with how quickly he had grown up and how much he knew about life.

"The last thing Uncle Beno said to me when they took us out of Chernovtsy was, 'Rudichka, you are the man now.' He looked so big in my twelve-year-old eyes. His wife, my Tanta Regina, hovered over me with sad eyes. I remember thinking I must have grown up overnight.

"But a year later, Beno's words followed me as I crawled through the Nazi warehouse and barracks in Mogelov. It was easy. The soldiers were either drunk or with women. I took what I could grab, flour, vodka, salt. I watched them through the windows when they raped our women.

"Some of what I took, we used. There were still cousins and aunts alive then, Grandma too. The rest I either gave away to the others in the camp or sold back to the Germans. Can you believe I sold them back their own stuff?" Rudy laughed. "You know who taught me that, right?"

I nodded. "It seems the gypsy girl taught you everything you needed to know before they took you away."

"Yes." For an instant Rudy had that faraway look in his

eyes, the one that made me feel alone. "So anyhow, everyone
had something to sell. The Germans only wanted to give me
marks. I got rid of those as fast as I could. I knew the Germans
would lose the war, that marks would be just paper. The others
laughed at me and shook their heads. What difference does it
make, they said, we are going to die anyhow.

"I was not going to die. I survived the sickness twice by the
time I was thirteen." Rudy would always bend over at this point
in his story and lower his eyes. "It was the typhus that made me
stronger, put the power in my arms, my legs, when I crawled
in the shadows."

"Terrible."

"Well, you know the Germans don't send me money for
nothing. When we finally got to America, the doctors in New
York examined me. They decided I had a nervous condition.
I had to squeeze something. Of course I couldn't do that. I
couldn't do anything they asked me to do."

"Couldn't or wouldn't?"

Rudy's eyes sparkled. "So they said I had a nervous disorder,
confused thinking, permanent. That's what they said. Typhus,
two times, poor man."

"Well, but you did have typhus two times. That should be
worth something."

"I know. Believe me, I know. I was blind for weeks after the
fever. They had to lead me around. And they gave us beans to
eat. You eat the beans and lay in your own, in your own shit.
Burning up and they gave me beans."

"And what about water?"

"Water?" Rudy looked up at the ceiling for a second. "She
wants to know about water." He looked down at me. "Forget
about it. Water, hah.

"I accomplished things no one would believe. And I was just

a little boy. Actually I was very little, and that helped even more. I kept them all alive. I disappeared into the shadows. I became one with the darkness."

Rudy straightened up and lit a cigarette. "In the morning everyone was looking for me. The big question was always 'Where is Rudichka? Did he come back?' Don't look at me that way. Yes, I loved it. I loved being so important.

"Things got worse. The German soldiers were getting bad news from the front. And of course they took it out on us. So one night I told my mother that she and I were leaving. The aunts, my cousins, Grandma were all dead by then. They froze, they starved, who knows anymore. It was just me and Mama and we did it. We escaped.

"Do you know how easy it is to hear voices in a cemetery, when it is just getting dark?"

"No, as a matter of fact I don't."

"We walked and walked, covering at least twenty kilometers a day and that's with stopping to retie the rags on our feet." Rudy closed his eyes. "I remember sitting on the frozen ground and wondering why I was wrapping those rags so carefully. After all, my feet were numb.

"We had lost track of the days, when we came to a deserted barn with a caved-in roof. I turned the hay over until the air was sweet with the smell of it.

"'Come back, Rudichka, don't forget me.' Mama Eva laughed and cried at the same time. I covered her with a horse blanket. 'I'll be back just like all the other times.' I wanted to cry too, but I knew I shouldn't. The last time I cried I was playing schmataball barefoot on the streets in Chernovtsy where I cut my toes.

"I got down on my knees and patted my mother's hair. I heard Uncle Beno's words. 'You take care of your Mama, Rudichka. You are a man now.'

"'Shah, shah, Mamala, sleep, rest yourself.' I bent over and kissed each of her eyelids closed.

"I whistled as I walked away. My breath hung before me in the frozen air. I came to a cemetery so I knew I must be near a village. I wanted to walk faster, but I had to slow down because of my feet. I concentrated on the weight in my pockets, the bracelets, the rings, the gold.

"People will say it was just the wind and that a hungry mind can play tricks on you, but it was then that I heard the voice. I forgot the pain in my feet. I ran. It was Grandma's voice trailing behind me. I stopped to catch my breath and looked around in the cold black night. She was dead. I knew it because I was there that last time she fell in the snow with her hand reaching out in a strange way. They didn't know right away if she was really dead, but I knew. If they thought her chest was going up and down it was because they stared too long. That's all. It was like the game we played in the camps, watching, staring until we made things move. Now her shrill voice screamed out, 'Don't go, don't leave me.'

"'Grandma, please, I have to keep going.' I tried to walk but I couldn't. 'Please let me go, we need something to eat. I'm sorry we left you. Please. Mama is dying. I need to find bread.'

"I was able to move again. The dark didn't matter, my feet barely touched the ground. And the pain was gone too. Faint voices swirled around me as I flew past tombstones that leaned into the frozen ground. I knew the pitiful baby sound was Manya's baby who didn't make it through that night that never ended. I tried. We all tried, covering her with our bodies, gathering into a tight circle to hold in our heat. In the morning we struggled to our feet and could only stare and listen to Tanta Manya scream. She tore her hair out as Mama and the others pulled her from the tiny blue body. A wolf howled somewhere behind us when we moved on.

"I was through the cemetery and on a dirt road where light from the cottages made it easier to see. Doing what the gypsies taught me, I found the friendly shadows and tiptoed to the last house, the one set back from the others. I hunched over at the side of a window to quiet my breath. A soft yellow light fell on the filthy rags tied on my feet. I let my body go and slipped silently to the ground. I closed my eyes and saw Mama in the barn. She was calling me. I jumped back up and peeped carefully into the window.

"Two children were perched on the sleeping ledge of the green-tiled oven. Their round cheeks were rosy from the heat. They were giggling.

"I was not about to be fooled. I knew who I was, even then. I knew who they were too. The people in that cottage would give me nothing, not a drop of water. They would watch me die of starvation or thirst right there on their doorstep. Then they would step over me, pausing only to strip my body before kicking me aside. How many times had I seen this happen? A beautiful young woman, burning with the fever, refused water because her parents had nothing to pay. Later, they came back to take her faded red dress.

"I pushed my hands deep into my pockets and caressed the gold. I loved the weight of it. I walked to the front door of the cottage and knocked hard.

"The door opened. Instantly I smelled the magnificent aroma of baking bread. I closed my eyes and took a deep breath, praying not to faint as the fragrance filled my head.

"The angry, suspicious eyes of the man before me were no different from the others. Behind him the wife stopped taking the finished bread out of the oven. Ripples of heat rose up from the high, shiny loaves; diamonds that glowed in the soft light. Remember I had not had food in days.

"I straightened my back, breaking the silence in my usual way.

"'I have something you want.' Easily, casually, in their own language is how I spoke. I pulled an item from my pocket, not even bothering to see what it was. It was more important to watch his face as the eyes lightened and became curious. The farmer stretched out his arm and stepped back.

"'Come in, come in.' His eyes did not leave my hand.

"I stepped into the room slowly. I heard the gypsy girl's voice. 'Don't look desperate. Don't look hungry. This man is not your friend. Do not trust him. Do not trust any of them.' I knew the only one to trust was waiting in the barn. There was no one else. Only this pig who must be bought.

"The faces in the room gleamed pink with health. For a second I wondered how they could be so untouched by what was happening only a short distance away. The room tilted. I knew if I fainted they would rob me and throw me out into the snow to freeze. I fixed my eyes on a small wood statue on a shelf. There was no mistaking the parted hair falling across the forehead, the bush of the mustache, the beady eyes bulging in their sockets. The room came to a sudden halt. Crying and fainting were for women.

"I remembered Mama's soft voice whispering to my Aunt Manya in those early labor camp days. 'My Rudichka does not know how to cry anymore.' They were squeezed into the corner of the bunker, pressed together to keep warm. I felt Mama's gnawing hunger, her cold. How could I cry? How could I tell her what was inside me when they kicked her like an animal? My tears were always there, only inside where you couldn't see them. As young as I was, I knew there was only one thing to do. Not to cry but to survive. Besides, the truth was my mother was right. I no longer knew how to cry. I didn't feel the hate during the day, but at night, unable to sleep in my space on the ground, my mind raced with the horror of things I would do when it was over.

"'Hush Eva,' my aunt had whispered back. 'He is alive, that is enough.'

"At the farmer's table I was in control again. I asked how much the bread would be as I looked around. I would have given all the days of my life to stay in that warmth. The dirt floor, the straw beds, the walls of dried cow manure were all we needed.

"An earring for two loaves was too high a price but I pretended not to know, not to care. The wife's hands moved slowly over the hot bread. She wrapped them, tucked in the edges of the paper. The farmer had many questions. Where did I come from, what was it really like, did they really do those things to the women, to the children? I clenched my teeth with the knowledge of what he wanted to hear.

"'You give me only two loaves of bread for this precious jewelry and information you want too? Look, this earring has a diamond in it.' It came out like a joke, but the farmer was hungry too. He turned to his wife and signaled with his head for her to wrap another loaf. I waited until she was finished before I leaned over the table. My face was close to his. He held his breath as if not wanting to breathe the same air as me.

"'To tell you the truth,' I whispered with a shrug, 'it wasn't so bad.' His mouth went slack. The sharp edges of hate were grinding in my stomach. 'Don't believe those stories you hear. See, look at me.' I stood up and smiled, puffing out my chest so the children could see. 'I'm all right, see strong, healthy. It wasn't so bad at all.'

"I handed him the earring. His rough hand closed around it. I almost grabbed it back when I thought about where it came from. But then I let it go.

"I stopped at the door to take one last look around and then walked out into the cold, knowing I would remember.

"The moon was gone. The icy wind swept around the cottage making me naked in its grip.

"'I'm just a little boy,' I said out loud to the wind. I raised the bread under my nose and sniffed.

"'Can I rest?' I asked. 'A piece of bread?'

"The wind continued its whine.

"'*Liebe Gott, wo bist du?* Loving God, where are you?'

"Silence. Someone back in the camp told me God answered children's prayers.

"Run, answered the wind, run.

"Seconds later the moon was out from behind the clouds. I ran. Stark outlines of tombstones and wooden markers welcomed me. I clutched the bread and slowed to a careful walk down the first aisle. It was the way the guards walked, strutting slowly, choosing, whistling the song with no melody. They were not afraid. Why should I be afraid? I studied how they walked up and down the rows of pale faces, how they smiled at the frightened women hugging screaming babies, the men staring at their feet. Lives. They were dealing with lives, made a game of it. I could do that. I turned up my collar like they did and laughed loud into the wind.

"The voices returned, frantic, screeching, wild.

"A crystal message carried in the biting wind wrapped itself around me, 'Run, Rudy, run.' It was then a great force lifted me, propelled me. The cemetery blurred and only that word pounded through my head. Run. A vague woman's form glowed in the distance, her finger pointing the way out.

"The drone of engines did not surprise me. German warplanes were coming from the opposite direction as I reached the edge of the cemetery. All was still except for the approaching thunder of them. What a beautiful sound the whizzing made. All the world was in slow motion as I turned and saw the first bomb light up the village behind me.

"I jumped over a low fence, landing on ground that rumbled under my feet. Mama's silhouette in the barn doorway flickered on and off like the movies they showed at the camp to visitors. The movies didn't fool anyone unless they wanted to be fooled.

"Mama ran across the field. We fell against each other, the bread squeezed between us.

"We were up and walking when the sun rose. A mist lifted over the tombstones. Mama stopped here and there, looking around. 'The spirits of the dead are leaving for the day.' Her serious voice comforted me. The early light illuminated markers that could no longer be read.

"Where the village stood, only small fires were burning. We passed a wall, a chimney. Perhaps I heard a child cry, but we did not stop. We walked. We did not see. We did not hear. How many times had we walked so, not seeing, not hearing our own people die.

"We came to the end of the village, to the last house. I crept into the smoldering ruins and returned quickly. I handed Mama two dark loaves.

"'Is this bread still good?'

"'Yes, Rudichka, it is still good.'"

CHAPTER 2

Rudy also brought his stories to the mountain cabin that I'd bought before I met him. It quickly became his retreat away from the city, too. He didn't say anything when I told him it was a sacred place, how I sat in my rocking chair in front of the crackling fire and let the spirits that lived there creep into my bones.

One of the first things I did when I bought the cabin was frame old family pictures and put them on the mantel. Grandma Bessie in sepia tone wore long golden earrings, thick lipstick darkened her lips. Her cheeks were heavily rouged. Though she was still young in that oval picture and looked pretty good, there was no denying Bessie smiled a wicked smile.

On his first visit to Mountain Lodge, Rudy examined her picture with his most serious face. "She is laughing at you."

"What for?" My sudden nervousness surprised me.

"She is laughing at you for thinking you can keep a gypsy like her in this house."

"I guess you don't know." My mother's voice came out of my mouth. "My Grandma Bessie was a very religious Jewish woman, not one of your gypsies."

"You must be kidding. Look at that face. If she is not a gypsy, she sure wants to be one."

"You're crazy."

Rudy threw up his hands in mock surrender. "You can think what you like. It is all right with me. But I know a gypsy when I see one."

Every Sunday morning Rudy went down the mountain for the newspaper and fresh rolls. He'd poke his head into the room one last time before leaving and wink. "I'll leave you alone with Bessie for a while."

Grandma Bessie's black eyes bored into me. I walked to the mantel and lit one of my perfumed cigarettes, the kind she used to smoke. A thick haze rose up to the loft and settled there. The aroma beckoned me to another place far away, in the same way Bessie did when she put me into those trances.

Before I was allowed to travel alone, I would go with my mother and Aunt Rosie to pick up Grandma Bessie for their routine Saturday shopping trip to the Fordham Road. There was one morning that always stood out in my mind. Grandma was in the bathroom putting on makeup. They kept calling out for her to hurry up. It always took her so long. I was at the white enamel table in her tiny kitchen playing with her cards, trying to teach myself to tell fortunes the way she did. The whispers in the next room were mixed Yiddish and English. I put the cards down and tiptoed to the doorway. I was only ten years old, but I understood a lot more than anyone knew, even Yiddish.

Aunt Rosie hissed, "It's her gypsy blood."

"I don't think you get gypsy blood that way." Mother's weak voice told me she wasn't sure.

"Oh yes you do." Aunt Rosie used her know-it-all voice. "He made her pregnant didn't he?" She was always making fun of Mother. Sometimes she even called her stupid. "He gave her a baby didn't he? That's all it takes."

"I still want to know who told you that? Papa would never tell you that."

"How many times do I need to tell you? Papa and Mama weren't married yet. They didn't even know each other. Papa told me everything in the nursing home. They all thought he didn't know it when he married her, but he did. That's why they married her off so fast, and so young too."

"But Mama's family was so religious. How could that happen?"

"I told you last time. When they realized she was pregnant, they shipped her off to Uncle Harry on the other side of Sadagura. They forced her to leave the baby there."

I caught my breath at the sound of that magical word I'd heard so many times in other family conversations, Sadagura.

"With Uncle Harry?"

"No, no, not with Uncle Harry, stupid. It was a shanda, remember? They gave the baby girl back to the gypsies by the river."

"Such a horrible story. I can't believe it. A Jewish girl falling in love with a gypsy. What a horrible story."

The springs squeaked in Grandma's couch. I moved silently back to the table and picked up the cards.

Mother's voice came closer. "But how sure can you be? Papa was always angry that Mama threw him out and wouldn't ever take him back. Maybe he was talking about someone else. Maybe he was confused."

"No. He knew exactly what he was saying. He even told me the year, 1924, the year that Papa and Mama came to America. Mama was fifteen years old."

"A gypsy sister."

"Well, don't worry about it. She's dead."

"Yes, I remember that part."

"Papa said there wasn't a gypsy left in Sadagura when the Nazis left. Not one."

Once I was old enough to cross Kingsbridge Avenue, I went alone to visit Grandma Bessie in her studio apartment under the elevated Woodlawn Express. I knocked, opened the door, which was always unlocked, and walked carefully across the newspapers put there to keep the floor clean. Most times I found her at the round table by the window studying her cards, the haze from her perfumed cigarettes enveloping her. Heavy gold earrings swayed on her stretched lobes. Grandma Bessie always wore makeup, except when she went to Schul. The day she died, at eighty-three, she was wearing bright red lipstick. They said her face was white, not so much from death as from the face powder she kept in a round silver jar in the foyer. She shopped for her bright, loose clothes almost daily.

Grandma Bessie always had money. I was sent to borrow some of it when my father had a bad night driving the taxi and there was no money for dinner. I lived in dread of those times. Mother gave me a note even though Grandma Bessie couldn't read. I had to stand in front of her and listen to her speech about my good-for-nothing father and how she warned my mother not to marry a cripple. Then she made me read the shopping list I was supposed to use at the A&P. She added up how much I really needed, reminding me that chopped meat was three pounds for a dollar and Del Monte tomato sauce was three cans for twenty-nine cents. With a box of spaghetti for nineteen cents, we could eat for a dollar and have dessert too. I always cried by the time I got to the end of the list.

Grandma Bessie marched to the shelf over her bed. She reached into a velvet purse and took out some coins. She jiggled them around in her hand while her gold rings winked and laughed at me.

"Come, chey, with your gypsy tears. Let me tell your fortune." She sniffed and wiped her nose with the back of her hand. She crossed her arms under her sagging breasts like she always did and lifted them.

She lit a candle, lowered the blinds, and pulled me to a chair at the table. Shadows played on her back when she stood before the mirror and wrapped a heavy silk scarf around her head.

Grandma Bessie's powder didn't cover the deep lines in her face. I kept my hands in my lap as her long red fingernails came toward me. I had a scar on my wrist from the time she grabbed me so hard I bled.

"Come, my little gypsy girl, give me your arm." She slipped the familiar gold band over my fist and up my arm. Her red lips moved slowly, forming words I didn't understand. The clatter of her false teeth blended with the clicking sound of the elevated train passing overhead. My eyes got heavy as the repetitive noise filled my brain.

I'm back again in the purple shadows. Leaves heavy with rain brush my face and arms as I pass through the forest. I turn the gold band as I walk by the river I know as Prut. I hold the rag ball on my hip, the ball made by the Gadjo boy. My feet do not make any sound as I look for him through the mist, in the bushes. Every day he comes. We play with his ball, but I do not give it back. Each time I let him find me in a different place. I know the gadje are dangerous, not to be trusted, but this one will be different. We need him.

First I taught him the patrin, the signposts we leave behind for others. Now I teach him Calo words, the words of my tribe. Father says they are borrowed words, borrowed from languages in countries where we left our seed and blood.

The Gadjo boy is younger than I am. The first time I brought him to the camp, the others did not notice us. He laughed when he looked down at the dirt floor. I motioned for him to lie on my blanket. I put more wood on the fire so the tent would get smoky. I heard my father's guitar, the loud laughter as the men passed the bottle. I knew the Gadjo boy heard it too as we dropped to the ground and rolled around. I slid my arms around him and pulled him to me. I lifted my skirt and put his hand between my legs. I wanted him to know.

The Gadjo boy comes to me every day. I teach him the things he needs to know. He brings us what we cannot get for ourselves now that we cannot go into the village. Some days when he is late, I look into my heart. I see that the Gadjo boy means more than a chicken or a gold coin. At the end of this month I must go to my father. I am old enough. I will bring the Gadjo boy to the circle. We will mix blood. He will be mine forever.

The sound of Grandma Bessie's movements brought me back. She opened the blinds as she hummed "Romania," the melody I knew so well from the records she played. Sometimes she'd dance in front of the mirror, shuffling her feet and lifting her shoulders while holding up her breasts.

Grandma Bessie's scarf was back on the hook. I went to the bathroom and sat on the bowl with my foot against the door that had been painted over so many times it would not close. Even though her bathroom was cleaner than ours, Grandma Bessie's bathroom wasn't really clean. She kept her newspapers in the bathtub. There was a line of burnt wooden matches on the edges of the sink and the bathtub and scattered on the floor. I knew she lit matches in the old-fashioned way to cover the smell when she went to the bathroom.

I was counting the pink and black tiles between the door and my foot when something warm slid out of my body. I grabbed hold of the doorknob and looked down at red water in the bowl and the blood on my underwear. I closed my eyes. This was it. This was what they giggled about when we changed for gym. I wanted to laugh. I cried. I took a deep breath, grabbed a handful of toilet paper, and stuffed it between my legs before pulling up my underwear. I flushed the toilet and tiptoed out of the bathroom, calling out goodbye to Grandma Bessie as I rushed toward the door.

She was there waiting for me.

"Goodbye Grandma." I looked down at the floor.

"Goodbye, gypsy girl." She put her hand under my chin and lifted my head. I couldn't look away.

"I have to go, Grandma, it's late."

"It is not late. It is early."

"Early?"

"Yes. It is just the beginning." Her eyes were shiny. She knew. I turned and ran out the door.

I couldn't believe that Rudy recognized who Bessie was from just her picture, until he started talking more about the gypsies in the camps, and especially those that lived in his town. When he heard how Grandma Bessie put me into those dream-like states, Rudy didn't look surprised. He just nodded like he knew it all along.

When she was dying, I drove to the Bronx every week to visit her in the Shalom Nursing Home on Kingsbridge Avenue. Those last weeks, she drifted back to the town where she left her baby. There was that name again, Sadagura. It sent magical gypsy blood coursing through my veins.

She thought I was her daughter, the one she gave birth to after she fell in love with my gypsy father. I asked her questions but she only cried, repeating over and over how sorry she was for leaving me to go to the new country. I told her over and over that I forgave her.

CHAPTER 3

One Friday night, Rudy and I arrived late at the cabin, as we usually did. We left my Jeep halfway up the mountain and walked the rest of the way under a starry sky. Bundled up in anticipation of the weather, I wore my high fur-lined boots, a storm jacket, and long underwear. Rudy, on the other hand, wore an unzipped cotton jacket over a shirt that was open at the neck. He said he couldn't be bothered with the extra gloves, hats, and scarves I kept on the back seat.

"Romantic, isn't it?" I said as he pulled me along through the snow.

Rudy turned and I saw a face I didn't see often. He blushed over the most ordinary things. Usually they were the very things I needed to hear the most.

"Yes. Very romantic." Rudy stopped. "And look at those stars." He looked up with wide eyes and an open mouth. "How come there are so many more stars up here?"

"It's a long story." I giggled as I used his expression. "Cute."

"Actually, there are so many stars tonight because we are here."

"Why didn't you just say so." Rudy's innocent look said he almost believed me. "Tell me again why we're doing this."

"Because ours is the last great love affair of all time?"

"Oh, right. I forgot."

In his more serious moments, Rudy said this was his last love affair with life. That night, in the dark after our lovemaking he sighed and compared our life together to his last soccer game, the one he never had a chance to play. "If this doesn't work," he whispered in my ear, "I hang up my shoes."

The next morning I made coffee and added wood to the fire. Rudy found some rubber boots and a red snow hat with pom-poms that hung over his shoulder. He had a way of putting it on, tilting it far to the side and making it look like it was about to fall off any second.

"One of these days you're going to lose that hat." I reached up and set it straight.

"I like risks," he said as he pushed the hat to the side again. "I like danger."

"Oh great! What a man."

I watched Rudy from the window over the sink as he marched down the path to get the Sunday papers. I remember thinking, as the red pom-poms disappeared behind a snow drift, if only it could always be like this.

I waited for him in the silence that only snow in the country can create, but I felt more than ever that I was not alone. Maybe it was because Rudy seemed to know right away. That first day, after studying all the other pictures on my mantel, he announced nonchalantly that we were not alone. Later he added his mother's picture to my collection.

It was in the cabin that Rudy had disturbing dreams that he decided were a result of the spirits. They were not like the nightmares he had in the bunker when he moaned and called out words that gave me the chills. At the cabin he would wake up trembling and go out onto the porch for a cigarette to steady himself. He said he was on a boat or a bridge, crossing, trying to cross over to the other side, but something was always wrong, holding him back. He'd shake me awake to make sure he was dreaming.

I always felt there might be spirits in the cabin, but once Rudy came into my life, what might be became, in my mind, what was. My head was so full of ideas that hadn't been there before, I didn't know where to start. My bookcase was slowly filling up with books about analyzing dreams, people who felt they had lived before, Nazis and concentration camps, and survivors. The more I read, the more I felt there was something big and important about to happen in my life, and that Rudy was going to show me the way. And so I waited. I didn't know what I was waiting for, but I believed it would come, that I would move from my mundane life to more, much more. Sometimes when Rudy talked about how he would take me home, to Chernovtsy, I would find myself filled with a longing I could not explain. Rudy knew enough not to call them gypsy tears when I cried. He nodded as usual and did not say anything. I felt he knew what he was going to do for me, even though I didn't. He said to believe, and I did.

Neo-nazis stared out at us from the front page of the newspaper Rudy brought back. His face showed no expression while he read, but the left corner of his mouth twitched slightly as he struggled with the words. Rudy had taught himself how to read English.

I hid my face behind my newspaper. "What do you think about that article?"

"Think? I don't think anything."

"You must think something."

"What should I think? You Americans have to think. You think it is all over. Big headlines, surprise." Rudy jumped up. His newspaper slipped to the floor. "Well, it is not over. It never was."

He walked to the fireplace and rested his hands on the mantel with his head down.

"What's that? What did you say?" I held my breath. "I can't understand your mumbling when your head's down."

Rudy turned slowly and looked at me. "I said, it is not over." His words hung in the air between us. He sat in front of the fire on a little red stool. The way his arms hung between his knees brought up that familiar, uncomfortable feeling in the pit of my stomach.

"What have I got? Look at my hands. Have you noticed my hands?" Rudy held out his hands as though I didn't know every line, every cut and crease. "Is this what you think my mother had in mind for me?"

"Look. That's the breaks. Isn't that what you always say? You taught me that. Remember?"

"Don't be cute. You know why I tell you that. I can't stand to see you suffer. I've done enough suffering for both of us."

"Okay, I know. But you were liberated, remember? You made your peace."

"You can't be naive enough to believe that. Look at me. Have you noticed? My feet remind me."

I turned my hot face to focus on the heavy evergreen branch outside the frosted window. The sun was at an angle that turned the melting snow into tiny, sparkling diamonds. One winked blue at me.

"And I don't have a son," Rudy cried out. "They took that too."

"Rudy, you don't have a son because, well, because you don't have a son. It's one of those things. I thought you didn't care one way or another. Remember? You told me in the beginning, you wouldn't want to bring a child into this lousy world. That's what you said. Didn't I say it was okay? Believe me, it's all right."

I walked up to Rudy and put my hands on his shoulders. He looked up. The web of creases around his eyes were deep.

"It's not all right. You know it's not all right. I am the last one. Don't you see how they robbed me? They took my family." Rudy looked over at my family pictures on the mantel. His eyes rested on his mother. "They took everything. They took the ring."

"The ring?"

"The ring. Don't you remember the story I told you about my mother's ring, my grandmother's ring?

"Of course I remember," I lied. "But you passed over the story so quickly when you told it to me. I thought you made it up." I did remember something about Rudy's mother Eva trading a piece of jewelry for a cup of water. "What's the difference now? They don't sell babies for rings."

Rudy struggled up from the stool. He paced back and forth in front of the fireplace. His hands flew in the air.

"That shows how much you know. The ring I am talking about was a family ring. Do you know what that means?"

"Yes. No. What does it mean?"

Rudy stopped. "It means that without that ring there are no sons. That's what it means." He looked into my eyes. "I need the ring. All these years, bad luck. Of course. Someone has it. I know they do. It's still there. Beno and Regina will help me."

"What good is it? Even if they did find the ring, how would you get it out of the country? Remember what you told me? They search Americans and their luggage for hours. You forget. Stop pacing."

"That's the point." Rudy's hands moved faster. "I forget nothing. They are morons. This is my last chance to make monkeys out of them. I want it back. It's mine. They've taken enough. It's not too late."

I tried to remember more of the story. The light from the fireplace made the wrinkles on Rudy's face deeper. He would grasp at anything now.

"Do you know what they would do if they caught us smuggling a ring out of their country?"

"Ah, but they won't catch us. I promise." Rudy stopped moving. "I will plan everything perfectly. I am smarter than they are. I was then. I still am. You will help me. You will get the ring out."

I hugged myself as the thought of a damp prison cell made me shiver. I smelled it. I pictured how the border guards would try to figure out his mixed-up accent, his suspicious passport.

"I will not fall into this insanity." I said.

"Well?" Rudy took a step and looked down at me as though he had not heard me. "Will you help me?"

"Yes, of course."

Later Rudy whistled while he lit candles in each room. Every few seconds he did a little two-step. The flames flickered and caught the shadows of the pine trees brushing against the windows. The maroon velvet couch still held the impression of our bodies from the last time when, hidden from the rest of the world, we listened to his gypsy music and sipped wine. It was always the best of times. It was then I knew the real Rudy. He spoke loving words. The lines in his face softened. His warm body relaxed.

Now I sat at the end of the couch and massaged his feet while Rudy talked once again about frostbite and his escape without shoes. I pictured a little boy shuffling through the snow, his blue toes. I hugged Rudy's feet to my breast.

He saw the tears in my eyes. "Now you know why I must go back."

"Yes, we will go back."

The passion of our lovemaking that night seemed startling to him, like it did every other time. He shouted, "Oh Mama," and laughed into the night air.

"Why do you laugh so? Are you laughing at me? Have I done something funny?" I made believe I didn't know the answer.

Rudy looked down at me with wet eyes, smiling the smile he didn't know he had. "Can't I laugh? Is it a crime to laugh?"

"It's just that I hardly ever hear you laugh like that. It's very nice. It would do me good to hear it more often."

He bent down and kissed my eyelids. His smile faded as he lifted himself up. Then it was gone.

So many times I wanted to cry out, "I hate you, I hate you," but it was what they did to him that I hated. A sadness settled inside me when I caught a glimpse of what Rudy might have been.

"Wasn't it enough?" He lay back and threw his arm over his eyes. His mouth trembled. "I gave you everything I had."

"Poor fool." I leaned over him. "You still don't know, do you?"

Rudy lifted his arm to block me. "I'm confused. I am a confused person, remember?" His voice cracked. "That's what the doctors said in the DP camp."

I heard a child. I saw a boy hunched up in a dark corner, crouched in filth, curled into himself. He wrinkles up and becomes an old man.

I kissed the soft spot between his shoulder blades. "It's all right Rudy, it's all right."

CHAPTER 4

Most of the time it was all right, with me trying to make him into someone else while Rudy just laughed and shook his head. He repeated over and over that he was a gypsy and when would I learn you can't just change a gypsy and expect him to stay that way.

One night he grabbed my arms and pulled me close to him. "You can't do this to me." We were standing in the bunker doorway. I tried to back up, to get him near the bathroom sink. His dark clothes smelled from the oil in his Brooklyn machine shop.

"Don't touch me." I snatched his cold hands and held them up. "Your hands are filthy." The light revealed his cracked skin caked with dirt.

"You still don't understand. The gypsy believes that as long as he is clean on the inside, the outside doesn't matter. You Americans wash and wash. It doesn't help. Americans are still gadje, dangerous, mahrime."

"Mahrime?"

"Yes, mahrime, unclean. Not you of course." Rudy's eyes sparkled with his quick response.

"Look at your hands. You talk about unclean. How can you come home like this?" I hung onto his hands for a moment. I wanted to hold them, warm them. "Where's your respect?"

Rudy looked at me with the familiar amused smile. I could not blame him. How many times had I greeted him this way? The way his hair fell into his eyes made it impossible to be really angry.

"Look at you. Look at your clothes. Why won't you let me mend that? And this place, this bunker." I threw my arms around trying to look dramatic. "Who would want you? I should have listened to my friends." My cheeks burned. "Your clothes are torn. You're filthy. For God's sake, go wash your hands."

"Maybe I want to keep people away like the gypsies do. Maybe I want them to be afraid of me too."

Rudy walked to the bathroom. I stood behind him. The soap glided through his hands. In an instant it was back in the dish.

"Do it better. Wash your hands again." Rudy's shoulders hunched. "They're your hands, damn it, don't you see them? So maybe you want to keep me away, too. Is that it? You want me to feel sorry for you? Yes, that's it. Now I've got it. Oh I know what you're up to."

Rudy looked up at himself in the mirror. Without rubbing, he rinsed his hands and turned to the towel.

"Look, look what you're doing to my towel."

"What? That was there. I didn't do that."

"Of course you did it. I just saw you. How can you say that? How can you lie like that?"

"Lie?" Rudy's shoulders dropped. "Did you say I was lying?"

"Yes, that's what I said." My voice faded to a whisper. Rudy turned. The fire in his eyes forced me to look down.

"Gypsies lie all the time," I said. "Especially to gadje, remember? You told me that."

"Get lost kid." Rudy's shaky voice filled the room. "Leave me alone." He pushed me out of his way and walked slowly to the other side of the bunker. He took off his clothes and curled up on his side of the mattress.

I sat in the corner and stared at his back. I imagined a little boy playing soccer on the cobblestoned street in Chernovtsy. His spindly legs barely touched the ground. His handsome face was alive with the game. He was smaller than the others but his head was large. When he bent to kick the ball, his smile was years ahead of him. His knowing eyes glanced quickly from left to right. I remembered passing a soccer field in Central Park where Rudy and I watched a boy of nine or ten playing football. His leaf of a body flew through the air.

"You see. You see how he is?" A wonderful excitement filled Rudy's voice. "That's the way I was, beautiful. I was a natural." He followed the boy with tearful eyes. "They took that from me too."

The clock showed I'd been sitting and watching Rudy sleep for an hour, but I couldn't get up. I pictured his mother, Eva, peeking out from behind her window, watching him play. Then I saw him only a year later, scratching the lice, the open sores on his legs, his hands dark with grime, cracked from the cold. There were potato skins on the dirt floor and a cup of beans. I smelled rotten meat. Rudy was searching for water, good water that would not start up the pain again. I saw a little boy darting in and out of the shadows, a shadow himself.

My rage subsided. I looked over to where he slept and saw the boy's face against my pillow.

In the morning Rudy got up quietly. When I opened my eyes he was standing in the middle of the bunker in the dim light, his hands limp at his sides. Today will be the day, I thought. Today he will leave without saying goodbye. But no, he walked back to our bed like he always did and got down on one knee. I turned away from the clean smell of shaving cream and toothpaste, groaning and pretending to be asleep.

"Schveetheart?" He ran his hand along my cheek and stroked the top of my head. "Still trying to change a gypsy?"

"That's sweetheart with a w."

"I'm sorry." He exhaled in what I knew was relief. He loved when I corrected his pronunciation. It was our joke when people tried to figure out where he came from. They would always repeat "Eight languages?"

"Well, yes," Rudy would answer, looking down at his feet modestly.

"Actually," I would add, "he only speaks seven languages fluently. The eighth one is English and you can see he's still working on that." That was one of our best laughs.

CHAPTER 5

Once I got a chance to tell him about my life, Rudy paid wide-eyed attention to the stories about my poor childhood in the Bronx. I was embarrassed to complain to someone who'd had a childhood like his, but mostly Rudy just smiled and said it was okay. I went on to brag about riding the subways at night in my struggle through graduate school. By the time I got to my miserable and childless marriage, I was sobbing.

"It's all over." Rudy pushed his handkerchief into my hand. "That's why I'm here, to give you a new life, to show you a new world."

"You sound like a genie." I laughed while I wiped away the tears. "But I'm really very independent. I don't want you to think I can't take care of my self. After what I've been through, I need to be my own person, independent, free."

"Look, I understand. Independence and freedom are the most important things to a gypsy."

Once again Rudy alluded to being a gypsy, and once again

I played along. I knew of course that he wasn't, although he certainly knew a lot about them.

I also made it clear from the very beginning that I would never marry again. Rudy said he understood that too, because he was like his king, that he would never marry until the end.

"The end?" I asked.

"Yes, the end. You see, during the day my king was the king. He lived in his palace. He was handsome and wise and did a pretty good job of running things."

"Oh, is that you?" I laughed. "Handsome and wise and doing a good job of running things?"

"No, not that part." Rudy stopped for a moment. "Well, yes, maybe some of it." Now he laughed too.

We were finishing dinner in an elegant harbor restaurant on City Island. The waiter was opening the second bottle of wine. I was getting used to Rudy's German check arriving on the first of the month and his spending some of his "shit money" as he called it, on expensive dinners. We dressed up, Rudy in his best blue suit and I in a special dress, the one he liked with the long, flowing skirt. He said I looked like the gypsy girl he could never have. He made me wear my hair loose.

Rudy had no regard for the day of the week or the food. All he cared about was that the restaurant had music. Rudy needed to dance. Once a month, positioned in a restaurant doorway in our finery, Rudy stood at attention, clicked his heels and raised his right hand. "Heil Hitler" he'd say under his breath. Only I could hear him.

That night in City Island was the sixth month in a row that we celebrated the shit money. "To my king!" Rudy lifted his glass for yet another toast. "At night he was a bum. He dressed in peasant rags and rubbed dirt on himself. He sneaked out into the village and got drunk as a bastard in the taverns."

"Yes, to your king." I raised my glass. "Is that the part that's you? Drunk as a bastard?"

Now we were laughing uncontrollably. Tears rolled down Rudy's cheeks. The people around us smiled.

Rudy bent over the table. "They are jealous of us," he whispered. "We are the last ones."

"Last what?" I pretended not to know.

"You know." The candlelight flickered in his eyes. "Well anyhow, so here was this bum, but the people adored him. So, one night, when he was drunk as a bastard, again, he met this beautiful gypsy girl." Rudy paused and put down his cigarette. I held my breath, hoping he would say what I needed to hear. "Every night he saw her and fell more and more in love. She had long black hair down to here." Rudy held his hands at an angle high on his chest just below his shoulders.

I tried to look away.

"Anyhow he gave up his kingdom and went to live with this girl in a gypsy camp by the river. They lived in her tent for forty years. And he loved her with a passion."

"A passion. Did you say a passion?"

"Yes, a passion. What's wrong with a passion?"

"Tell me what do you know of passion?"

"Don't tease me." Rudy looked down at the floor in mock sorrow. "I have feelings, you know. Nobody believes it. I have a heart like everyone else."

He looked out over the water. I waited. Say it, I thought. Say it, damn you.

"So," Rudy continued, "they were getting along just fine, but the gypsy girl wanted my king to marry her. She was always begging him. My king never said no. He'd say, "Someday," and laugh."

"Like you laugh?"

"I guess so. Well after forty years, my king was old and sick. He was dying."

"And he kicked the bucket and never married her?"

"No."

"He went home to his castle to die in luxury?"

"No. As a matter of fact he felt guilty. He called a priest, and on his deathbed, on the last day of his life he married his gypsy girl."

"Nice story. However, that can't happen to us. We've already established that. Remember?"

"True. But in case you change your mind, remember, I am like my king."

CHAPTER 6

Rudy planned what was to be our first trip to Chernovtsy, his home. The city had been part of Romania when Rudy was born there but was taken over by the Soviet Union after the war. On that first day at Shady Nook when he said he would take me home, I thought he was crazy, but after a few months I started to say we were going home. By the time we were ready to leave, I did know almost everything about his family in Chernovtsy, especially about his Uncle Beno and Tanta Regina.

"They were like my father and mother," Rudy said. "My mother was pregnant with me when my father, Poldi, died of tetanus from an accident on the trains. After I was born she stopped talking. My first memories were of how she sat by the window, how she didn't do anything. I remember how Uncle Beno bent over her, calling her in a gentle voice. 'Eva, Eva, Eva.' She didn't answer. She just stared out the window. You Americans have a word for it, I don't know. She stayed like that for years.

"Every morning Tanta Regina rushed to our apartment after finishing her own work. She aired the bedding out the window. She bustled around the kitchen preparing food for her sister-in-law and her nephew Rudichka. She coaxed my mother to eat. Another one of my earliest memories is of Regina brushing out mother's long hair. 'It's going to be good, Mamala,' she chanted. Regina's voice made me safe.

"On winter mornings I climbed down from my bed over the oven. I pulled over a chair and struggled up to the high windowsill. Then I sat there straining to see Regina's round shape appear at the corner. My great fear was that she would not come. If she didn't come I would die." Rudy's voice filled with a rare emotion. "I would freeze up right there on the windowsill in my nightdress with my knees pulled up under my chin while mother watched me silently from her corner.

"But then there were those warm summer days when Regina brought us to her backyard on Ivan Beguna to get fresh air. Beno put up a swing for me. He was a plumber and he came home everyday for lunch like all the men did. I played with my soldiers in the grass and looked up to see him at the iron gate, watching me. His bright red cap always looked like it was ready to fall off. He waved and called out 'Rudichka.' That was enough. I was proud to be strong enough to pump the water when Beno washed. Regina served him at a wooden table set under the tree.

"While he ate, he spoke to my mother as though she heard him. 'Well, my dear Eva, how fine you look today. And with color in your cheeks too. Regina,' he called back to his wife in the kitchen, 'did you put rouge on my shvesta today? She looks so healthy and strong.' Mother did not smile. She never did.

"A day stands out in my mind. Regina bustled around her kitchen preparing Beno's lunch when suddenly the sky darkened. I ran around the yard catching the huge, warm raindrops in my mouth. Regina was trying to pull my mother out of her chair. Just then Uncle Beno came into the yard. In one smooth motion he lifted mother up in his arms and carried her into the house. He sat her in his own big chair and called for me to get a towel. 'That's a good boy,' he kept saying as I patted my mother's arms and face and hair. 'That's a good Rudichka.' He smoothed the hair on my head. 'You will always take care of your mother, no Rudichka? Remember. Always remember.'"

CHAPTER 7

Belgrade, Yugoslavia 1977

We weren't supposed to be in Yugoslavia. We were supposed to be in Chernovtsy, but our visas had been denied at the Russian Embassy in New York with no reason given. I didn't dare say anything, but I felt it was because of Rudy's fake passport with the wrong place of birth and birth date.

Rudy had saved up a lot of money by then. It was mostly gambling money, but I didn't say anything about that either. Five immense suitcases packed with gifts and medicines for his family were lined up against the wall of our Belgrade hotel room. To make matters worse, Uncle Beno wrote that Rudy must come as soon as possible. Rudy's old Aunt Regina was ill and asking for her Rudy. Rudy decided we should get closer to Chernovtsy and try again.

On our first morning in Belgrade, he hurried off to the

Russian Embassy while I was still in bed. He promised he would be back with the visas by noon. Rudy said he waited all day, but in true Russian style, nobody came.

He paced back and forth in front of the gated building, smoking one cigarette after another. The sign outside said they would open at nine.

He burst back into our hotel room like a madman. "Bastards."

He banged the bathroom door, threw himself on the bed with his arm over his eyes, then jumped up again. "They can't tell me what to do. They can't say no to me. I'll show those Nazi bastards. I'm not a dog."

"Show them what? When did Russians become Nazi bastards?"

A short laugh escaped me. "I mean, it's hopeless. Maybe next year we'll get in."

"What do you know about next year?" Rudy's voice was harsh in a way I rarely heard. He poured a shot of vodka in a glass and swallowed it.

"Hey, take it easy. It's not my fault. You don't have to talk to me like that."

Rudy was trying to make a knot in his tie but his hands were too shaky and he gave up. "You think I don't know you put a hex on me?"

"You're joking, right?"

"No I'm not joking. I know your tricks. How many times did you tell me you wouldn't come here with my dirty money? Huh?"

The streetlights were just coming on when I turned away and tried to focus on the avenue below. I crossed my arms tight across my chest and used all my strength not to cry.

"See, you're quiet now." he said.

I could tell he was talking through his teeth. He had an uncanny way of walking without making a sound. Now he was right behind me.

"You're a damn nut case." I took a step closer to the window.

"Get away from me."

"Say it's true. You wished this on me." Rudy grabbed my shoulder to turn me around but I pushed his hand away.

"Don't touch me."

"You'll be sorry." He walked to the closet and pulled out the dress he'd brought home for me before the trip. It was one of those slinky dresses, maroon with gold threads running through it. I hadn't worn it yet but I did try it on and knew it looked terrific on me.

"Get dressed." He threw the dress on the bed and reached up for my sandals.

"It's too thin. You can see right through it."

Rudy's head snapped up. He threw the sandals on the floor, one at a time.

The pain on his face made me sorry for my words. "You can see my underwear," I said in a lower voice. I knew that refusing a gift from Rudy was the one way to hurt him the most.

"Then don't wear any underwear. Who knows. Maybe you'll meet someone with clean money." Rudy walked to the door. "I'll be waiting in the lobby. A man by the embassy was handing out cards for a new club that just opened. We have a reservation. He said tonight they will have the best gypsy music in Belgrade."

"I thought you were upset. How can you go out like this?"

"They can't break me. I'll dance like the gypsies did. I'll show them."

"Rudy?"

He didn't turn around. "What?"

"Do you really think I put a hex on you? I mean, do you really think like that?"

"Yes. Gypsies do it all the time."

"Son of a bitch," I yelled when he slammed the door behind him.

I stood naked in front of the mirror. "Maybe I'll do just that," I said out loud. I put on panties and slipped the dress over my head. I stood sideways and saw how the light behind me filtered through the silky material.

I put on extra makeup and then the gypsy earrings Rudy loved.

When I reached up to pin my hair on top of my head, my breasts rose under the dress.

It took a while for the taxi driver to find his way. There was no sign to indicate a restaurant on the dark back street in the Starigrad, the old city of Belgrade. The loud gypsy music coming from a brightly lit cellar helped.

Rudy took my hand to help me out of the taxi. "This is it."

He slipped his hand under my coat and felt around just long enough to see if I was wearing anything under the dress.

I didn't have to ask if he forgave me for the hex, or for anything else. Rudy's anger never lasted long, at least not the anger he showed.

The club was smoky and crowded. Rudy nodded and answered in his most arrogant voice when the host asked about reservations. A waiter clicked his heels and took my coat. I heard the word "impossible" when Rudy pointed to a table in the far corner, but then he pulled a bill from his pocket and slipped it into the waiter's hand. As we walked across the floor, everyone turned to check out the Americans. There was a brief lull in the music, and then the gypsies started to play the "Star-Spangled Banner."

"Oh God," I moaned. I raised my voice so I could be heard over the music. "How come they always know?"

"Schveetheart," he whispered in my ear, "it's the dress." He pressed his hand against my back and moved me along to our table.

A moment after we were seated, the owner arrived to say he was honored to have his first Americans in his new restaurant. Rudy spoke in a conglomeration of all his Slavic languages. He ordered the mixed grill, always the mixed grill, and then the best wine in the house, always the best wine in the house.

The "Star-Spangled Banner" was over and the lead gypsy, a wrinkled man in a colorful bolero started a sad tune on his violin as he moved slowly toward our table.

The wine hadn't come yet when Rudy stood up and unbuttoned his jacket. He held out his hands and tilted his head. "Would you like to dance?" The way he crinkled up his forehead always made me think of a boy asking a girl to dance for the first time.

"Is this music we can dance to?" I asked.

"All music is music we can dance to." He moved my chair back and took me in his arms.

We didn't walk to the dance floor, we hardly ever did. Dancing next to our table was how Rudy created our own world wherever we were. He moved with his usual grace and with the detached look on his face reserved for dancing. He looked cool, but his heat, mixed with his cologne, emanated in waves from his body. The excitement of dancing with him always made my knees weak. I looked up at his face. I could barely remember that other man in New York, the one in oil-stained clothes whose hands left smudges on the walls of the bunker, and who handled a bar of soap like it was on fire.

I pressed my thumb against the softness between his stiff white collar and his ear. He reached over in his distracted way to pat down my hair as it brushed against his chin. My waist tingled from the tight hand that led me, controlled me through a tango and made me into a worthy partner.

"He sings from the heart."

I pressed my body against him. "At least he has one."

"Schveetheart, don't start up again."

"That was a pretty bad scene in the hotel room."

"But look where it got you." Rudy planted an exaggerated kiss on my forehead. "Here you are, naked under that dress, the center of attention and who knows. Maybe someone will ask you to dance, someone with clean money." Rudy laughed at his own joke.

"Sometimes I think that's what you really want. Is that what you want?"

"Do you know what he's singing?"

I rested my head on Rudy's shoulder and sighed.

"He's singing about freedom, how he loves freedom and is free to love. That part's about how he gave his gypsy girl her freedom."

"And where did it get him?"

"Can't you tell? Listen. He's crying."

"I suppose now we'll start talking about the value of suffering again."

"I wouldn't dream of it." Rudy looked over my head at the old gypsy and winked.

He invited the musicians over when they took their break. He had already finished one bottle of wine and ordered another one for the gypsies. He knew gypsies never drank while they worked, but he didn't know that I knew. Rudy started his usual banter. I understood when the gypsy asked Rudy, San tu Rom, are you a gypsy? Rudy laughed without answering and told him their music would make them millionaires in America.

Rudy had enough wine by then, but I had given up trying to

stop him long ago. With each drink he moved away from me, from Chernovtsy, from Beno, from Regina, from everyone and everything. I could tell he was asking the old gypsy if he'd been in the camps, and which one.

Just when I thought I no longer existed, Rudy looked over and beamed. "Schveetheart, we're pralos, he's my brother." The two men embraced.

"That's nice." Perhaps the sparkle in Rudy's eyes helped because I was successful in not sounding sarcastic. I studied how their shoulders touched, how white Rudy's hand looked next to the gypsy's.

There were five gypsies in all. The one sitting next to me was about thirty-five. I felt his eyes on me as he moved closer and added more wine to my glass. I ran my finger around the rim of the glass and thought about whether I was uncomfortable. The warmth from the wine spread through my body and stopped between my legs. His dark curls fell over his forehead and his skin was the color of my morning coffee when I had added just the right amount of cream. For a second I thought about that coffee, how I needed it, how I savored that bittersweet taste, and how it brought me to life like nothing else did. I thought about the gypsy man, how I could savor him and let him make me come alive.

He moved closer, just a bit, but enough for me to smell the starch in the shirt that was stiff against my arm. I looked up into his laughing eyes.

He asked a question across the table. Rudy raised his hand and waved. He didn't lift his head, or stop talking with the old gypsy, but I knew that wave. It brought back memories of cold, angry times when he couldn't care less what I thought or did.

I called across the table, "What did he ask you?"

"He wants to know if he can dance with the American woman, if it's okay."

"Well, what did you tell him?"

Rudy waved his hand again. "I told him American women can do what they like." Rudy turned his head away. "Actually, I told him you'd love to dance with him."

"Wait, how can you say that? You didn't even ask me first."

"I didn't have to."

"Well, what's his name for God's sake?"

"Zigone." Rudy shouted back. "Just call him Zigone."

The gypsy man smiled with startling white teeth. He moved my chair back. I waited for him to reach out, touch me, but then I realized he would never do that. He followed me to the dance floor. The other gypsies took their places and the music began.

In one motion I kicked off my sandals and pulled out my hairpins to make my hair wild. The gypsy was on one knee in front of me, waiting as I raised my hands over my head. I smiled down at him and said, under my breath, "I'll show him."

I didn't care that anyone who wanted could see my naked body through the dress. The music started slow, like it always did. The flame inside me grew as the melody quickened, and the gypsy man's glazed eyes followed my breasts. He was no longer on one knee but squatted with knees far apart. He leaned back on one hand making the material of his pants stretch and I saw the outline of what was beneath it. His other, extended arm brushed against my dress as I swayed.

Two other gypsies joined us and the three men danced around me in a circle. I turned my body away from the corner where Rudy sat. I was afraid to see that he was not watching.

I was wild and angry from the smell of my own body. Bastard, I hissed to myself. I glanced quickly over my shoulder.

Rudy sat there alone, watching me through a haze of smoke. His elbow rested on the table. The tip of his thumb was against his clenched teeth, a familiar pose.

I couldn't help myself. "Rudy, come dance with us."

He shook his head and took a deep drag on his cigarette.

"Good!" I called back. "I'm free! I'm beautiful! They love me!"

When the music stopped, I thanked the gypsies and started to walk off the dance floor. They laughed and begged me to stay. I ducked under the table for my shoes but they were gone. I stood up and hesitated. This might be my last chance ever.

I saw the frozen smiles on the gypsies faces and I knew Rudy was behind me even though he hadn't touched me or made a sound. He bent over and kissed my cheek. "Having fun, Schveetheart?" He was holding my sandals.

"Yes, of course. This was the best . . ."

"The best what?"

"Well, you said have a ball, didn't you?"

Rudy waved the gypsies away. "Yes, I did." He took my arm and led me back to our table.

"You're hurting me," I lied.

"Sorry." He loosened his grip on my arm.

"It's okay. I know you can't help it. It's the jealousy, right?"

"No, I've had too much to drink, that's all. And so have you."

"For God's sake, Rudy." My voice was too loud. "Just once," I spun around and hit him on the shoulders with my fists, "Just once I want to hear you say you're jealous."

He lowered my fists.

"You're too God damn cool." I rested my head against his chest and wailed over and over, "I hate you."

"Quiet, shah. I'm not that cool." He stroked my hair and buried his face in it. "You've just got a lot to learn, gypsy girl, although . . ."

I lifted my head. "Although what?"

"Although that dance you were doing. How did you know that dance?"

"What?"

"The Tanana." He pulled out my chair. "I've only seen it danced two times but I remember it."

"Well, I wish I could say I knew what I was doing, or what you're talking about, but I don't. Sounds great though." I bent down to put on my sandals. "So I was dancing the Tanana. What steps did I take that made you think about it?"

"It's not the steps. It's the eyes."

"Whoa! I like that." I lifted my water glass. "To the Tanana. Long live the Tanana, and to jealousy!"

Rudy lifted his water glass. "To my gypsy girl, who dances the Tanana. So, what did you learn tonight, gypsy girl?"

"Mmm?" I didn't want to answer.

"Well?"

I saw myself in the middle of the dance floor, the gypsies in a circle, clapping and looking up at me. "I am an American woman. I learned that I can dance all I want, with anybody I want."

"That's true. But I was hoping you realized what that Zigone was thinking."

"What difference does it make what he was thinking? He didn't even touch me."

"See that! That gypsy knew everything about you. What you know about him is like a drop in the ocean compared to what he knows about you."

I remembered the outline under the gypsy's pants. "Well, I guess . . ."

"I know what you're going to say." Rudy's face was suddenly pink. "Forget it. The Tanana is about as close to having sex as, as having sex."

"Oh Rudy, don't get carried away. That's not what I was going to say!" My voice wasn't very convincing. "Next thing I know, you'll be saying I was unfaithful for just dancing like that."

"Unfaithful?"

"Yes, you know, like," I lowered my voice and pretended to sound mysterious, "like fooling around."

Rudy kissed my hand and didn't say anything for a few seconds. "You know what the gypsy says about being unfaithful."

"I don't want to hear this one."

"Sure you do." He let go of my hand and placed it on my head. "The gypsy says that if his wife has sex with another gypsy, even looks at another gypsy, she is unfaithful." His hand closed into a fist. "The punishment is pretty bad too."

"Nothing unusual about that." I froze. "Maybe we should go now. Look almost everyone is gone."

"I'm not finished. But if his wife has sex with a white man, for money, she is not being unfaithful at all."

I straightened up. "Oh, I know!" I threw my hands up in the air. "I know!"

Rudy's voice joined mine. "It's just another way to earn a living!"

The musicians were taking another break, so our uncontrollable laughter filled the quiet room. The remaining people looked at us and smiled, like they always did.

"They're jealous too, you know. You will have to get used to it. I can't say I blame them though."

"I know! People are always jealous when gypsies have fun."

Rudy signaled to the waiter for my coat. "Come, gypsy girl, I'll show you fun."

CHAPTER 8

By morning, Rudy had resigned himself to being stuck in Yugoslavia for a while before making another visa attempt. By late afternoon, we were racing through barren countryside in a rented Mercedes, looking once more for gypsy music.

"I would think you'd had enough last night," I sank back into the soft leather seat.

"Enough music or lovemaking? Doesn't matter. I'll never have enough of either one." Rudy laughed at his own joke. "Anyhow, the gypsy music in the next village is supposed to be even better than in the Starigrad."

"Sometimes I wonder about you. You really have a thing about these gypsies. What are you really searching for?" I didn't dare ask if it was really their music he was looking for or the gypsy girl he never had.

"What's there to wonder? Thousands of gypsies were murdered in the camps. Of course the authorities bragged they were trying to save them, and us, from the death camps in Poland. Can you believe it?"

"Yes, I believe it. I also believe you had better slow down or there'll be police behind us any minute. It's raining you know."

We had been driving for hours in blinding rain and fog, through rocky mountain tunnels, around curves with sheer drops down to the Adriatic. Rudy's brave face didn't fool me.

"An adventure," he called out in a shaky laugh. "You are my co-pilot. Your job is to encourage me, talk to me so I won't be tempted to look down into the sea."

"Aren't there any speeding laws here?"

"No one follows the laws here."

"How do you know?"

"I know. No one follows the laws here, so the government makes more laws. And no one follows them either." Rudy slowed down. "One thing about those gypsies, nothing could stop their songs, their music. Even when we got off the cattle cars. The gypsy knows what it's all about."

"And I suppose they taught you what it's all about."

"Yes, as a matter of fact they did. You don't want to hear about it, remember?"

"And I still don't. So what were you doing while they danced and sang?"

"I watched." Rudy threw back his head and laughed again.

"Be serious. Watch the road."

"It was cold." Rudy shivered. "Do you know that the gypsy makes forgetting an art?"

"How do you know what he remembers and forgets?"

"I know everything."

"Everything?"

"I know a gypsy spirit can conquer death."

"Like the Jews?"

"No, not like the Jews. They make an art of remembering."

"And you?"

"I remember those broken-down boats they put us on to cross the Dniestra River." Rudy's voice was suddenly flat. He glanced over at me and then back at the road. "But it's a long story."

"I have time."

"Ah, there's the village. There is no time. We have to find a hotel. I can tell you this much though. When we got to Transnystria, my mother didn't bring me orange juice in the morning like yours did."

"I don't believe it. You still sound angry."

"And that surprises you?"

The harsh edge in Rudy's voice stopped me. I leaned over and whispered, "Why do I love you?"

He grasped my hand and held it over his heart. "I don't have the slightest idea."

Mysterious old Sinj appeared out of the fog. The narrow streets built centuries before cars presented a new challenge. Rudy parked up against a stone wall. I crawled out his side of the car. We splashed through alleyways hoping for someone to come along. Dim streetlights did little to light the way. My mouth watered from the smell of fried fish coming out into the street. The sides of the buildings were damp and green with moss. I stood still to catch my breath. Rudy walked ahead but then stopped and looked back.

"What's up? Keep moving. It's raining. I'll find somebody."

"There's no one here. It's dinnertime. I'm hungry."

Rudy walked back to me. "You know, kid, you would have never made it. I'm sorry to say this, but you would have never made it."

"Why do you always say that?"

"I just want to tell you that you would have never made it. That's all."

"So you made it. Bravo. Look at you. You call this making it? Look at us, dragging around in this downpour looking for gypsy music. Who would believe it?"

"Believe it." Rudy put his hands on his hips and cocked his head. "Maybe I just want to see if you can take it."

His wet hair was plastered to his forehead. A drop of rainwater hung from the tip of his nose. Above his head a pot of geraniums on a warped shelf sat close to the edge.

"What's so funny? Maybe you are right." Rudy shook his head. "Maybe this is too much for you."

"It's those geraniums." I pointed up to the shelf. "I pictured them falling on your head."

Rudy looked up behind him. He took a step away from the side of the building and grabbed my hand.

"The girl's losing it," he called out as he pulled me along.

A few minutes later, we realized we had made a circle and were back at the car. A little pension with ornate iron balconies overlooking the fishing boats was behind the car and old stone wall. The soothing sound of water slapping against the dock promised a peaceful night.

From our covered balcony I watched Rudy walk back for the luggage. He struggled in the rain to get the lock open. A man who looked like a tourist stopped to help him. Rudy gestured and pointed in response to a question. The man stepped back. His question had probably been answered and he was getting wet. Rudy put his hand on the man's arm and continued to talk. The man said something and tried to shrug Rudy off. Rudy held on and kept talking. I wanted to look away. My face burned. I understood him so well. He had someone to talk to.

Just a few minutes before, he had rushed around the room checking the closets, the balcony. He grabbed me and kissed me hard on the mouth. "I am so happy here. This is perfect."

"We deserve it after that ride."

"Let's make it our own. Now. This minute."

"Wait," I giggled. "I need time to wash up."

"I want you this way."

I pulled away. He threw his hands up and mumbled something about American women. "Okay then, I will get the baggage. But you have one minute to do whatever it is you do."

I was already half undressed as I walked him to the door. He looked back at me, paused for a second, and then he really looked at me. I held my breath waiting for him to say something about how I looked. He never did. But then he did that Zorba thing I loved.

"Don't forget me," he said in the sing-song voice. "I won't forget you," I sang back. He kissed me on both cheeks and ran down the steps like the young man I pretended he was.

Now he stood in the relentless rain. The baggage sat in the mud while his hands flew about, drawing ridiculous maps in the air for a stranger.

"How dare you," I said out loud. I wanted to shout down to him, "How dare you keep me waiting?" The trembling and passion from a few minutes ago had turned to rage. How much I could hate him always surprised me.

Why, why, why, I asked myself. I could lie to myself and say it was his smile, his tears, his weakness. That it was the way his hair fell in his eyes and how unaware he was of how handsome he was. I could say he was a boy whose growth had stopped fifty years ago, a boy who needed me, a guide to keep him alive. Could I believe that I stayed with Rudy just for the glory of knowing how he looked when his defenses were down, how his lips parted and how tears squeezed past the corners of his tightly shut eyes when he called out, "Mama, oh Mama"?

I turned from the balcony and closed the glass doors against the chill and fog. To hell with him.

I labored with the cork on the champagne bottle he was saving and started to cry in little gasps when I realized I couldn't get it out.

There he was, knocking on the door.

"Go away," I shouted.

"What's wrong with you? Let me in."

"Go away, I said. Go back and stand in the rain." Silence. I heard him thinking this over. I always heard him thinking.

"Are you a damn gypsy?" he asked whenever I told him what he was thinking.

"It's possible," I answered, using one of his own, favorite phrases. "Anything's possible."

Now I read his mind from the other side of the door. Stupid. He didn't even know why I was angry. I took a deep breath and wiped away my tears. I opened the door.

"I thought you forgot me." I said.

Rudy looked at my tear-stained face and then down at his feet. "I did not forget you."

CHAPTER 9

Our austere room in the old but spotless pension had a rose garden that filled our bedroom with perfume. Glossy, painted white furniture that would have been odd elsewhere was perfect here. Handmade lace stretched over our bed, hung from the windows and covered the oval table in the corner. There were two slices of dark bread and a block of salt on a gilt-edged plate next to our bed. Rudy asked the shy girl who brought us a snack what the bread and salt were for. He raised his eyebrows and tilted his head.

I waited until the door shut behind her. "Well?"

"A local custom, for luck . . ."

"Sounds good to me."

" . . . for the newlyweds. It seems we are in the honeymoon suite."

I eyed the food the girl brought, hard boiled eggs, salami, fresh rolls and a clear cold bottle of unmarked vodka. "Let's pretend we're newlyweds." I lifted my glass with the token vodka Rudy always put in it.

"Schveetheart, I wouldn't know where to start. Better yet, let us toast to the last of the world's greatest lovers, as you say. To us. Na Zdorovie!"

"To us."

When we got to the restaurant later on that night, I was heady from our walk down winding streets. Leaning buildings seemed to almost meet above our heads like cathedrals. The rain had stopped and a smiling moon made it seem almost light. A soft breeze lifted my skirt.

Rudy looked down at my legs. "Why don't we take off our shoes?"

"What about the stones?"

"You get used to it. Remember?"

We sat on a wooden bench. My heart ached at the sight of his long white feet resting on the cool stones next to mine.

Tinny opera music flowed down from a balcony where an old woman watered red flowers in a blue window box. Rudy's voice was unusually gentle when he called up to greet her in her language. He called her Mama. Faces peeked out from behind curtains to watch the Americans pass. Barefoot children in shorts twittered behind us, singing silly songs Rudy pretended not to understand.

At the restaurant, Rudy was drinking enough for both of us. I laid my hand over his before he lifted each glass and pointed out another fishing boat coming in from the black sea.

He looked briefly over his shoulder at the light and nodded. "Coming home," he said before he freed his hand.

The gypsies knew all the melodies Rudy wanted to hear. The oldest musician, who was perhaps seventy, wore a faded red velvet vest trimmed with gold braid. His crisp white shirt contrasted with his wrinkled, coppery skin. His sad eyes fixed on Rudy, who slipped more and more money into the strings of the violin. I loved the way Rudy cocked his head to one side when he really listened; the violin spoke only to him.

It was late and, as usual, we were the last guests. Rudy begged for more music but the gypsies dropped their instruments, sighed in unison and gestured they could no longer play. Rudy's eyes filled with tears.

"Are you happy now?" I asked.

"Yes, of course. Can't you see I'm happy?"

"I know, but the gypsies see your tears."

"Oh, they know."

"They know what?"

Rudy bent over the small table and beckoned me with his finger. "They know that when a gypsy cries, he is happy."

Rudy wove down the street on the way back to the pension. It was almost funny how his English was mixed with all his other languages when he had too much to drink. His jacket was thrown over his shoulders with the collar turned up.

"You look like a soldier." I raised my hand to fix his collar, but he pushed it away.

"Doesn't it excite you?"

"No," I lied. "It does not excite me."

"Liar." He stopped under a streetlamp and pulled me close to him. "Do you still like me, Schveetheart?"

"I think so," I giggled. "Yes I like you."

"Even though I am who I am?"

"Well, you did give those gypsies too much money."

"No, no, not that. You must know by now."

"Robbed a bank to get money for this trip?"

Rudy ignored my attempt to make him laugh. He gripped my arms. "You really don't know, do you?"

"Stop shaking me."

"You don't know me." Rudy looked down, catching himself as he started to fall.

I reached up to that soft spot behind his ear. "Of course I know you. I know everything about you."

"Then you know?"

"Rudy. You're very tired. Let's go to bed."

"You said you knew me. Remember, you just said it. But I . . . do you think it's easy? I bet you think it's easy, to go on living, knowing what they did. Knowing what I did."

"Let's go. We'll talk in the morning."

"No, now."

"Please, in the morning, I promise. Besides, you're hurting me."

"Now." Rudy's hands said there was no stopping him from what he had to say. "I had to do it. By the time the Russians came to liberate us there was nothing else to do. The Germans knew what was coming. They ran off that morning. But they left their wounded behind."

"Tell me at the pension, come."

Rudy looked over my shoulder. "The Russians marched through. We stood behind the wire and watched them. Mama said it was okay to cry. We were all crying and shouting and laughing. The Russians threw guns on the ground, shovels, axes. It was so easy to bend down and grab the handle of that ice pick and pull it under the wire."

Rudy leaned on the streetlamp and slumped down to the sidewalk. His cheeks were wet. I bent down to take his hand but he pulled away.

"You can't take it away now. It's mine."

"Rudy, it's me, look. It's me, see?"

"Yes, it's you. I know who you are." Rudy's nose was running.

I reached down to wipe it, but again he pushed me away. "I know what you did. I saw you with them, with my own eyes. Damn you, see, teeth don't come out that easy, do they?"

"Rudy, please." I tried to pull him up. "Come on with me, please."

"Good. Beg. Now it's your blood." His face twisted into a horrible grin. "Slowly, slowly. Scream. Go ahead. I can't hear you." Rudy's high-pitched laugh echoed down the street.

"Shhh, Rudy. Please. Shhh. Come."

"Bleed like a filthy pig."

Rudy struggled to his feet and leaned on me. I was shivering and crying as I pulled him along. Finally there was silence except for our footsteps.

We walked through the misty garden and up to our door. Rudy sat heavily on the bed and fumbled with his clothes.

"You're too drunk to undress."

"I can do it." His nasty laugh was new. "And I can undress you."

I lifted his feet onto the bed. "Shah, shah, go to sleep." I wiped beads of perspiration from his forehead with my hand.

"No. I need you."

"You've had too much to drink. It's useless. Besides, it's my time of the month." As the words came out I realized immediately I'd said the wrong thing.

Rudy sprang up. His feet banged to the floor. His arms locked around my waist. A cold sweat formed on the back of my neck as his upper arms squeezed me. I squirmed as he kissed my stomach. The muscles of his forearms fastened to my hips.

"Let me go. Please."

"It's too late."

"Just let me go to the bathroom. I'll be back in a second. I promise."

"It's too late. Now."

"Don't say that. You're hurting me."

I tried to pull myself out of his grip as his mouth moved lower. His teeth and muffled words pressed against my body. I didn't need to understand his words to feel his rage.

"Swine," he cried out. "See the blood. I will do it to you like you did it to them. Beg. Don't stop." He jerked away and snorted, making a shrill animal sound that brought back those nightmare nights in the bunker.

In the mirror behind him I watched myself hit his back with my fists. "Stop," I cried as his head moved lower.

I stopped struggling as we sank to the floor.

His eyes darted about the room. "I have to give it to you," he repeated in English and German. "I have to." He crashed down with all his weight. "Burning," he whined. "Do you smell them burning?" Rudy threw his head back. His nostrils flared. "Skin, can't you smell it? Hair."

His tears fell on my breasts.

"Bubba," he cried out to the darkness. "This is for my Bubba. And this is for Manya," he sobbed as he moved to a new place inside me. Then it was for Schimel and for Leah, and for Zeda, and Ruza, Emile, Yoel. I trembled from the smell of tobacco, of alcohol, but from something else too as I rose up to meet him with the same animal wildness. Our sobs mixed in the space between us. Then, in one cry, he called out "Mama," and then, in German, "Loving God, where are you?"

I stayed awake listening to Rudy's soft breathing.

The moonlight coming through the lace curtain settled on the edge of our bed. I sat up to pull the cover over us and brushed against his foot. Its coldness shocked me. "Oh, Rudy."

"Mmm??"

"I love you, poor Rudichka," I whispered.

He reached for my hand and pressed it over his heart.

CHAPTER 10

We woke bathed in sunlight. Rudy was as fresh and happy as I had ever seen him. He mumbled something about the great music and was getting out of bed when he stopped and asked me, like he always did, if our lovemaking was okay. I answered, better than okay, like I always did.

We went downstairs to an outdoor café where the waiter snapped a crisp white cloth over our table. The hanging copper pots of the shopkeepers around us caught the sunlight. We sipped espresso between bites of brinza cheese, tomatoes and tiny black olives. Rudy broke off small pieces from the crusty warm bread and put them on my plate. Around us the Starigrad, the old town, came alive with vendors and the call to prayer from a nearby mosque. A guide walked backward across the Starimost, the old bridge. He threw his hands out toward the turquoise water in a grand gesture, and the group of tourists facing him all sighed. I rested my chin in my hands and closed my eyes to the sun.

Rudy broke the silence. "There she is!"

A boy in a torn shirt and a girl in a long ragged dress clutched her brightly colored skirt as the gypsy woman approached our table. A baby made gurgling sounds from the limp canvas sling suspended around the woman's neck.

She reached out to Rudy. "Please, please," were the only recognizable words.

Old women dressed in black were washing the street. The wet stones at the gypsies' bare feet sparkled.

I bent over and whispered "Look at their feet, so dirty."

"You would be dirty too." Rudy answered in his most sober voice.

"And look, the little one, he's shivering. No shoes, they have no shoes. Rudy."

"It's all right." Rudy waved his hand. "You get used to it. I walked like that for five years. You get used to it."

"You get used to it? You know you don't get used to it. Don't you still get frostbite after all these years? You can make your excuses. The kid's cold."

Rudy searched his pockets. He cursed under his breath in feigned anger as he dropped coins into the gypsy's skirt.

"Is she allowed to beg like this?" I looked around to see if anyone was watching.

"This is not begging. Remember?"

"I remember already. 'It's just another way to make money.'"

Rudy and the woman exchanged strange words before she suddenly whirled away, her brood grasping her flying skirts. Another sling sagged across her back.

Rudy's blank face was impossible to read. "Did I ever really tell you about the gypsy girl?"

"You know you haven't. I don't want to hear this story about your gypsy girl. All the tourists are out. Let's go look at a mosque or something."

"You do want to hear."

"Why are you saying it like that?

"Because you need to hear. It's time. What if I told you my gypsy girl fits in with your story about your Grandma Bessie?"

"There's a fine excuse." I tried to sound sarcastic. In a flash I went back to our first meeting, how the air got still when Rudy read my palm and said he knew me, how he talked about Romania and gypsy tears.

"When I was a boy, the gypsies lived under the bridge by the River Prut, between Sadagura and Chernovtsy."

"Sad . . . agura?" I tried to roll the *r* like he did. The name sounded familiar.

"Yes, they camped there to have water for themselves and their animals. Besides, people didn't want to see them, which seemed fine to the gypsies. They came into town only when they had to. The men staggered under the weight of the vegetables hanging over their shoulders. Their women came to tell fortunes."

"Could they really tell fortunes?" My voice was dreamy as I followed bright dots that danced behind my eyelids.

"Depends on how you look at it. A gypsy can read your face, even read your heart." He took a breath. "So they came to town in a confusion of noise and color. Their children followed from a distance, disappearing into the shadows to steal chickens. I can still hear my mother's words when she bent over me and put food in my plate. Her mourning for my father took years, but once she was well she started cooking again. She made the most wonderful goulash, and from scraps too. I can smell the garlic. How that spicy sauce made my mouth tingle."

"What about the gypsies?"

"Oh, so my mother would always tell me, 'And remember Rudichka, stay away from the gypsies. They steal white boys like you.'

"It was a summer afternoon right before the Germans marched into Chernovtsy. I was finally old enough to go along with the big boys to play soccer, we called it 'futball.' My feet were cut and bleeding from playing on the stones in the street."

"Shoes?"

"Enough with the shoes. It was hot that day so we went down to the river, the River Prut. Chernovtsy, ah. It was beautiful in the summer. You know I don't remember walking. I see myself skipping everywhere. We pulled off our clothes and left our schmataball in the grass. We splashed around, making a lot of noise. I remember the icy water on my body. I was free. I was a big boy."

I laughed. "To think you were once a boy."

Rudy looked at me with indignation. He sighed and lit another cigarette while signaling the waiter for more espresso.

"How old were you?"

"Maybe ten. Can you believe I was ten? No, I was eleven. The Germans hadn't come yet. So I came out of the water refreshed. The sun was going down and we were fooling around with the ball again, kicking it lightly from one to the other. Futball was my life. I couldn't get enough by then. I knew I was good. I got carried away and hit the ball so hard with my head that it flew up and into the bushes, way back from the river. The boys accused me of showing off. 'Look what you've done,' they yelled. They threw on their clothes and left me there alone to find our precious schmataball. I started to cry. Boy was I scared."

"You, scared?"

"Don't laugh. What do you know about schmataballs? Do

you know how long it takes to make one? Schmataballs are made from schmatas, rags. Do you know how long it took us to get enough schmatas together? You have to wait for your mother's old stuff, stockings and worn-out rags. Let's put it this way, I wasn't going home without that schmataball. I tried to go around the bushes. The thorns ripped my arms and my bare legs.

"I felt eyes watching me, but I knew it was my imagination. I kept my head down and whistled. I tried not to look to the side, but then I had to. She was there, watching me, smiling."

"Are you telling me you remember her smile?"

"Yes, because it was the kind of smile you know, even as a child, is not quite right. I wanted to run. I tried to run. I remember thinking 'run,' but I looked into her shiny dark eyes and it was too late. She reached out and there was a ring on every finger. The gold bracelets on her brown arm sounded like little bells."

Rudy slouched in his chair. The morning sun played across his face and his half-closed eyes.

The sounds of the Starigrad faded away. The familiar pain in my gut reminded me how much I loved him. "I don't want to hear the rest of this story."

"She had the schmataball on her hip. I hear those bracelets now, the gold against gold when she moved her arm, beckoning me to come."

He paused again. I sank back and closed my eyes. It was so easy to see the whole scene.

"I was born that day in the purple shadows by the River Prut." Rudy's voice blended with the tinny radio music coming from the café.

"Purple shadows?"

"Yes. So I followed the motion of her body. She made no sound. Her long colorful skirt dragged along the grass."

"Did she wear shoes?"

"Stop with the shoes. No shoes. Do you know why gypsy women wear long skirts?"

"I'm afraid to guess."

"Gypsies don't like the sight of a woman's knees." Rudy sat up and looked into my eyes. "There were gold coins woven into her hair. Her black hair hung down to her waist, sort of like this." Rudy made voluptuous circles around his head and shoulders to suggest how the gypsy's hair fell.

"I know. I know, enough already." It didn't matter. Rudy didn't hear me.

He lay back again and crossed his legs. He put his hands behind his head.

"So tell me."

"So her hair was down to here." Rudy demonstrated again.

"I know, for God's sake. Get on with it."

"First you have to understand I was not an ordinary kid. I was a little man, a midget. As a matter of fact, that is what they called me. Times were different then too. There was something in the air, like a dark cloud forming. I had to grow up fast. I knew more about life when I was eleven than most adults today. At least I did when she got finished with me."

I tried to look away, to focus on something else. I couldn't.

"It was her eyes, deep, black. She led me back to her camp, to her tent. It was away from the others so no one saw us. Besides, there was a celebration going on. I heard a violin, a guitar, they were singing and shouting. The girl stood me in the middle of the dirt floor. She looked me over with her hands on her hips. Then she threw her head back and laughed in that way only a Tzigone can, a laugh that makes you forget who you are, where you come from, everything. Do you know that to a Tzigone, the greatest sin is not to laugh?"

I didn't answer him. I could hardly breathe.

"Well, that is what they believe. It is a sin. And of course, they even laugh when they are suffering."

"What?"

"Yes. That's how they survived. Well, so, I laughed too. We fell to the floor and rolled around like we had been overtaken by a dybuk. There were colorful rags and clothes thrown about. Big pillows and carpets were piled in the corners. I smelled the horse tied outside. And she, she had got herself a white boy to play with.

"She caught me and crushed my head tight against her breast where I rested to catch my breath. She put my hand there, then on her belly, then between her legs. She made me do things, with my fingers first, in that wet place, then with my mouth. She moved down and I felt the hot breath inside her mouth and her teeth.

"Her smell was everywhere. Her blazing eyes hovered over me as she pushed small hard nipples into my mouth. And all the time she was laughing, mumbling in her strange language.

"I fell back panting. Her warm hand still rubbed my dusty, scratched body."

Rudy made me as excited as I'd ever been. He bent over the small table and reached out for my hand. "Ah, look at you."

"I told you I didn't want to hear it. I knew it would upset me. And I could've lived without all those details."

"Look how flushed your cheeks are."

I pulled my hand away. "It's the sun. It's stronger now. Can't you see that?"

"Oh, is that what it is?" Rudy called out to the people on the street in some language.

"What are you saying? What did you say to those people?"

"I told them it's the sun."

Rudy's laughter made people look over at us. Crazy Americans, I could almost hear them whispering to each other. Then I couldn't help it and I started laughing too.

"Come." In one fluid movement Rudy threw a handful of coins on the table, grabbed my hand and brought me back to the pension.

He sat in the corner of the room on a velvet throne-like chair and waited for me, his amused smile visible through his haze of cigarette smoke. It was too early and the water was still turned off from the night before. In desperation I grabbed the bottle of mineral water next to our bed and took it behind the flowered screen.

"Hey, what are you doing back there?"

"Trying to wash myself. Oh, it's cold."

"You'll get used to it."

Rudy's husky voice made me weak. I slipped his shirt over my naked body and closed a button. "This water is too cold. I have to wait until the water goes on. You'll have to take me the way I am." I came out from behind the screen.

"That is just the way I want you." Rudy walked across the room. "Here. Wrap this around your head." He held out the gift he'd bought me a few days before in the old market. Bright yellow fringes hung from the edges of the vibrant red and blue scarf.

"Why?"

"Because I want you to. Do it. Just for today. You will look like that chey, that gypsy girl up there." Rudy gestured with his head toward the gilt-edged painting.

"Are you kidding?" I didn't move.

"Here." Rudy crushed his cigarette. He wrapped the scarf around my head in his clumsy way, fixing the long fringes over my shoulder. "That's good, that's good." His eyes sparkled. His breath bathed my face.

"It doesn't take much to make you happy, does it?" I moved closer.

"See, gypsy girl." His hushed voice embraced my ear. I stared at my image in the mirror. Rudy took my hand and pulled me to the couch under the painting.

"Shhh," Rudy whispered. "Someone will hear you." He pushed me back.

"I don't care much." I giggled. "You're just afraid someone will hear how an American woman can enjoy herself. Are you jealous?" How I hoped again he would answer yes.

He didn't answer. He never did.

I lowered my voice. "You're making me crazy."

"No." He pressed warm lips against my stomach. "No, not yet, I will show you crazy."

Rudy bent over me. I reached up to brush away the hair falling in his eyes. He kissed my hand before moving down.

"Harder." I lifted my head to watch him.

"I don't want to hurt you."

"Why do you always say that? I love it. Please."

"Like that? You like that?"

"Do I have to teach you everything?"

Hot breath penetrated my breast. "Like that? Is that good?"

"You know it is." I stretched down and moved my hand to the rhythm of his mouth, caressing his smooth skin.

"Please," he begged.

"I can do better than that." I pushed him off. He fell onto his back. I glanced over at the gypsy girl in the painting on the far wall. She sat on a stone ledge. Her lover held a guitar and looked up at her longingly.

"What would your gypsy girl do now?" I teased.

"You know, you know." Rudy put his hands behind his head.

"Are you the king?"

"Do what she would do."

"I don't know, show me." I rested my cheek on his stomach and trailed my finger up his thigh, around his stomach and back down the other leg.

He groaned as he reached down, grabbed hold of my hair and pushed my head lower.

"Yes, oh Mama, yes."

Later he covered me with a fur throw from the back of the couch. "Good morning, my gypsy girl."

"Tell me my name," I demanded. "I want to make sure you know who you've just made love to. I'm not your Tzigane girl, you know."

Rudy looked down and kissed my eyelids. "I know who you are."

We propped ourselves on the many pillows. Rudy pulled up the quilt when the shy girl brought in a tray with salami and wine, peppers and bread.

Rudy balanced the tray on the bed. "Now I will tell you why I will be forever grateful."

"Grateful to whom?"

"To her, to you, what's the difference? It started with a chicken."

"A chicken? Oh, how romantic."

"Yes. She taught me how to steal a chicken." He gave me a bite of the peppers he'd put on a slice of bread. "I bet you think you steal chickens in the morning."

"Well, actually I never thought about it."

"You steal them in the evening when the farmer is tired and finished for the day."

"I'll have to remember that." I sipped the wine from his glass.

"So, after a while I went out on my own and brought back what I could steal. It was getting more difficult for her people to go into town. Everyone lived under that black cloud I told you about, and they blamed everything on the gypsies. It didn't take long for the others to know me. I was important to them."

"I thought you couldn't speak to each other."

"At first we couldn't. But her people knew some Romanian and she taught me words in her language. After some months, the Balubasha, their leader, announced I could be with them. He was also her father. They still called me Gadjo, their word for a non-gypsy, but they knew they needed me. I have to admit, the people in town did have reason to fear them. This tribe was descended from the Laeshi, once the most dangerous tribe of all. They were tall and dark with eyes as black as coal.

"One day I asked about her mother. She shook her head and grabbed me. She struggled with me, pulled me down on top of her and forced me with her strong arms to pump my body against hers. Then she pushed me off, squatted on the ground and squeezed out an imaginary baby that she picked up and rocked. She wiped the tears from her eyes with one hand while she acted out how the mother had walked away from the baby, far away over the water."

"How sad. It sounds like her mother was raped."

"Yes, but no. It seemed that her mother had a love affair with her father. She also gestured that her mother had white skin like mine. I guess that explained why her skin was not as dark as the others. But she didn't allow me to feel sorry for her. When I reached out to touch her shoulder, she pushed my hand away and wrestled me to the ground, laughing."

"A sin not to laugh."

"Yes. And yet, other things they did not consider sins. For example, the gypsies were known for their cheating. They would set up a deal and always, somehow, get the victim so involved he didn't know how badly he was being cheated, especially at fairs where they doctored up the horses. Then there was their passion for gold.

"It was their eyes. They fixed on you and cast a spell around you, fascinated you, could make you do almost anything."

"What about your mother? Didn't she wonder where you were all day?"

"I don't remember what I told my mother. The mood at that time was so distracted that she hardly questioned me. She was probably glad to let me go wherever I went to be out of the way.

"So, the gypsies practiced their own kind of medicine. I learned about herbs. They also interpreted dreams, worked charms. They knew what you were thinking. They knew what you felt. One of their tribe, I remember his name, Goru, was in."

"In?"

"*In* was what they said when they meant jail. He was in for stealing a horse. They wanted to move on but they couldn't leave him. They couldn't go into town to get him either. Goru was only in for three months though the usual time for this crime was a year. Even the townspeople knew that you couldn't keep a gypsy in for as long as a white man. A gypsy dies if he is kept in confinement too long." Rudy laughed. "That is, if he hasn't managed to pick the lock or make duplicate keys.

"A gypsy must be free. Love and freedom are all he needs to survive. They had this song. It had to do with worldly goods. You could think you possessed them, but they really possessed you, and could even destroy you. In the song, love is compared to the blowing wind."

I looked up from the plate balanced between my knees. "Is this you, Rudy? Where is this coming from?"

Pink rose up in his cheeks.

"And you're blushing, I don't believe it."

"It's me. So anyhow, you know how the wind is fresh and brings life? Well, if you capture the wind within walls, it becomes stale. In the song, there are open tents and open hearts."

Rudy sipped his wine. A great black bird circled in the sky outside our window. "It's important to let the wind blow."

His deep, serious voice made my skin tingle. "Yes, yes of course."

"So, I became their middleman in a way. I brought them everything I got my hands on. Food, gold. I think they knew the Germans were coming. Even I, too young to know of such things, knew something was going on. I felt it in the streets of Chernovtsy. Everywhere people were whispering. The currency changed so many times. But the gypsies taught me. Always it is gold."

"You didn't get caught stealing like that? How did you do it?"

"I can't remember except that I was absolutely under her spell. I lied. I told any story I could."

"Like you're under my spell?"

"Sure, like I am under your spell." Rudy tried not to laugh but he couldn't hold it in.

"Say it like you mean it."

"I mean it. So one night I jumped out my bedroom window and made my way to their clearing near the Prut. The men were sitting in a circle passing the bottle from hand to hand, from mouth to mouth. By then I was able to greet them in their own language. It wasn't easy. Gypsies don't really want you to learn their language. Oh, I knew some words but there were so many that meant the same thing you could never learn them all. I learned many other languages in the camps but none were as difficult as theirs. They borrowed words from every language. She told me that in exchange they had left their seed and blood. Seed. I thought that meant they left plants behind."

I closed my eyes and saw the clearing, heard the music. "Left behind seed and blood?" My voice echoed from somewhere else. I opened my eyes and hummed a melody.

Rudy didn't look surprised. "Yes, that's the music. So, it looked like they had found something new to celebrate. They were always celebrating."

I stopped humming. "I know they were celebrating."

"Why are you repeating everything I am saying?"

"I'm not repeating what you're saying. You're repeating what I'm saying."

"Okay, okay, so they were celebrating, like I said. And the music was fantastic that night. The music in Eastern Europe now, almost all of it, is really gypsy music. And the violin that night, ah, it could tear your heart out." Rudy put his hand over his heart. "Even now, when I hear a gypsy violin I am right back to that night."

The shy girl knocked to take the food and plates away. Rudy made his sign for drink. I usually hated the way he stuck out his little finger and tilted his hand toward his mouth. This time was different. Everything was different.

We waited for the next bottle without speaking or moving. The gypsy girl in the painting looked down on us as the shy girl poured our wine.

We clicked our glasses together. There were no words to say. I rose up from the bed and stretched before I moved behind the screen to wash. The bed squeaked when Rudy got up. His clothes made a comfortable rustling sound as he dressed. He whistled the same tune I had hummed a few minutes before.

CHAPTER 11

Sophia-Moscow Express, February 1978

"You hear? They are telling them I am coming home." Rudy threw his head back and laughed. Tears rolled down his cheeks. Each time the whistle blew he held the curtain aside and gazed out at the frozen villages that flew past. Our train hurtled through the night, bringing us from Bucharest to Chernovtsy.

I sank into the faded red velvet seat and sipped hot tea from a glass in a silver holder. I envisioned myself in a vintage film. The warm air in our compartment lulled me into a dreamy mood where Rudy and I were the last of the great lovers, on the last of the great trains. Rudy reached over and spread his trench coat over me. He tucked in the ends like he always did.

The gentle rocking, the haunting voice of a man singing a Russian song at the end of the car enveloped me. A shrunken old woman moved through the corridor as her straw broom scratched along the carpet. She turned a dried-apple face toward our compartment. She smiled a toothless grin and nodded before she moved on.

"We made it Schveetheart. Finally." Rudy gently slid the door shut. "I am taking you home."

I didn't have the heart to remind him that we weren't there yet. I smiled and snuggled down further into his coat where I could smell him.

A loud knock jolted me awake and I sat up and banged my head on the upper berth. Border guards jumped into the train while it was still braking. We were rushed into a smoky border station where metallic clanging and shouts of "Americansky" echoed.

White frozen breath formed when Rudy exhaled. His head turned slowly as he counted the pieces of luggage around us. He raised his eyebrows in the mock nonchalance I knew so well.

Three hours later the border guard motioned for me to get back on the train without Rudy. Inviting yellow light shone through the steam billowing up from under our sleeping car window. The cold from the thick ice penetrated my boots as a brutal gust of wind wrapped my coat around my legs and almost knocked me over. It was three o'clock in the morning.

The guard touched my arm and shouted over the wind. "Hurry Americansky, the train, she goes."

Rudy had warned me many times this could happen, that he would be more suspect than I. Damn his mixed-up accent and that passport saying he was born in Germany. I remembered his confidence and how his strength had propelled me to this moment.

"You think about things too much," he scolded when I lay next to him in the dark making mental lists of things that could go wrong. "You Americans, 'Go for it,' you say in your films, in your advertisements. 'Go for it.' But you do not go for it. You talk, talk, talk. I will teach you what it means to go for it. I will make you untouchable. They dare not come near you. They are afraid of American women. You'll see."

There was that day on Delancey Street, a few months before this trip. Rudy shopped for my wardrobe, bargaining with the shopkeepers. Later, our foreheads almost touched as we bent over steaming vegetable soup. "You're crazy," I said as I chewed on rye bread and blew on my spoon. "Do you know you're crazy?" Rudy looked up at me and grinned.

His craziness had become mine. First he convinced me that this could be done. Then, that it must be done. Somewhere in the process he slipped from calling Chernovtsy his home to our home. Eventually he said only that he was taking me home.

On nights when he had an extra drink, his deep voice lulled me to sleep as he went on and on about the frozen baby, gold teeth, typhus, bread, diamonds, and then the ring. In my dreams I saw it all. I saw them waiting. Once his obsession became my own, his excitement lifted me beyond thought of risk, beyond sanity.

The wind stung my eyes with splinters of ice. I turned to look behind me at the rough concrete building where they had taken Rudy for questioning. Rigid guards formed black shapes before the barren snow-covered fields. Is this the way it was? Is this why he made me swear?

"Do you swear?" he had demanded. "Say you swear. Say 'I swear I will go on no matter what happens to you.' Say it." Rudy bent over so close I saw the yellow flecks in his eyes.

"Okay, okay already, I swear."

"You're not taking this seriously. You are not even looking at me. Say it again. Look at me."

"I swear."

Now my heart pounded in my ears as panic set in. I turned back again. A faint outline of the building was all I saw through the snow coming toward me.

"Rudy," I cried. "Rudy, I can't . . ."

The pressure of the guard's hand on my arm intensified. I glanced once more at the train and took a step back just as his head shot up. I looked over my shoulder and saw Rudy running toward me through the snow, his open jacket flying in the wind. He was waving and shouting. More guards ran behind him, carrying our suitcases. Rudy slipped on the ice just as he reached me. I caught him and we jumped onto the train just as it started to move out of the station.

CHAPTER 12

Chernovtsy, USSR, February 1978

Regina's faded housedress hiked up in the back, exposing legs thick with blue veins. Swollen feet encased in homemade flannel slippers held her large frame. Her black and gray hair pulled back from her round face accentuated gold teeth that glittered when she smiled. Her upper lip was crowned by a faint mustache. When she threw her massive arms around me and crushed me to her breast, I was a child again.

Rudy stood in the corner, shifting his weight from one foot to the other until it seemed he could contain himself no longer. He stepped up to Regina's side. She wiped her hands on her soiled apron before Rudy took hold of one hand, bent at the waist and kissed it grandly. He clicked his heels and then holding her hand high in the air declared, "Here with great pride, I introduce you to the most beautiful babushka in all of Chernovtsy, my Tanta Regina." Regina beamed. She kissed him on both cheeks and also crushed him to her breast. Regina called him Arma Rudichka, poor little Rudy, as he looked down at the floor with a shy smile. She fussed over him, kissed him and patted his arms and head, as if to make sure he was really there.

In another corner Beno, too, waited his turn with tearful eyes. He told me, through our state-assigned interpreter, "You see, our Rudichka has not forgotten us." Beno wore Rudy's clothes that were sent over the many years. Although about six inches taller than Beno, Rudy was otherwise an exact younger version, with the same high forehead and tight mouth, which now trembled with emotion. Beno was also shorter than Regina. I loved them both instantly.

I took advantage of them talking all at once to look around Regina's dismal kitchen. The scene included a sink like the kind used in America for a laundry sink. I found out later Regina could coax the four-foot-high refrigerator to hold enough food for dozens of people. Rags hung from nails on the wall next to a green-enamel, three-burner stove. There was a wooden table covered with oilcloth that had long since lost its color and pattern from scrubbing, and, in the far corner, there was a daybed.

After the initial excitement subsided, I never again heard Beno and Regina speak out loud to each other. Rudy said it was their great respect for each other. Their hushed, whispered voices made the most mundane things seem their own little secrets. They shared a cramped, four-room apartment with at least half a dozen relatives at any given time. My understanding of Rudy and his way of being deepened as I watched how Beno and Regina created their own world within a world. I thought about the world Rudy so successfully created in our bunker, on the porch in the mountain cottage, even when we danced in a discreet corner of a restaurant.

Beno and Regina perfected their hushed and whispered communication so well that even at close range they could not be understood. When Beno sat at the table, Regina hovered over him using her large body as a shield. He barely needed to lift his head. She bent down close to catch his words. "One mind," Rudy said with unfamiliar admiration in his voice. "Beno and Regina don't need to talk to each other."

That night, Rudy, Regina and I sat at the kitchen table. The reminiscing turned to the ring and Rudy's mother. Regina asked if I knew about it and Rudy told her no.

"Do you want me to tell her the story your mother told to me?" Regina asked.

"Yes, please." Rudy's voice was unusually sober. Regina moved her chair and faced me. She proceeded to do all the talking while Rudy, sitting with his arms on the table and his head down, translated.

"We sat here, at this same table, Eva and I. I know exactly what year it was. Eva and Rudy's father, Poldi, had just arrived from Pulawy, from Poland. It was 1928. She was so young and full of life. She said it was important that I remember her story well, that I keep the letters she sent me, and so I have. And now I read them to you.

"I was about to become a bride, so my mind did not dwell on the fear in Papa's voice that night. It had started with the usual whispering under the oil lamp when he and Mama thought we were asleep. The words *ghetto*, *beatings*, and *separated families* brought me back from my half-sleep and wedding dreams. I already knew about the atrocities from the teachers who passed through our village. They told us stories from where they slept

in the loft over the oven, but these things could not happen
to us.

"Nine children we were, eight after Beno left, so we made
up a class of our own. Papa worked on the trains, and there was
always a teacher for us. Sometimes Mama slipped into the back
room to listen. I'd turn and there she was in her babushka and
apron, her rough hands crossed over her chest as though she
was praying. She looked like she held her breath so as not to
disturb the lesson.

"The other parents in Pulawy sent their children out into
the countryside, or even the next village to earn a few groshes.
In our house it was different. Before dinner, Papa stood at the
end of the long table and reminded us that food for the brain
was much more important than food for the stomach. And so I
learned three languages. I read every book and paper the traveling teachers brought with them. By the time I was ready to
marry Poldi, I felt I had visited all the world from my shtetl.

"His family and mine were neighbors all along. Poldi was
my first love. We were always expected to marry, only now our
wedding was rushed. Our families would leave Poland as soon
as the weather turned warm.

"The last winds of March blew through the slits in our
synagogue's wooden walls during our ceremony. I shivered in
my thin dress with only Mama's good wool shawl to protect
me. Poldi shivered too in his borrowed suit. Everyone crowded
into the small space and clapped when he stomped on the glass.
The old women sighed and wiped the corners of their eyes
with their aprons.

"There was no privacy for newlyweds in town, so a horse
and sledge waited to take us up to the shepherd's cottage. We
huddled in the back of the sledge, wrapped in animal pelts. The
driver flicked his whip and the horse started his slow trip up
the mountain.

"I remember how the old man winked when he shut the cottage door behind him. We were both virgins.

"Poldi pulled the straw bed in front of the oven, where we could sleep and be warm. He pressed me into our warm place, then prepared the soup and toasted bread and cheese on the fire. He fed me like a child. We giggled so much. Our laughter and love spread to every corner of the cottage. It pushed us together until we were one. We came down from the mountain filled with hope in the sons we would have in the new country."

Regina stopped reading. She folded the letter and put it back into its envelope. I had avoided looking at Rudy, but now when I did, his pale face was filled with pain.

"We will stop here and eat." Regina sighed and stood up. "We will go on to the next letter after we eat, no?" Rudy nodded and she proceeded to bustle around the tiny kitchen.

He picked up the thin letters and gently turned them over and over in his hands. He didn't say anything. He didn't have to.

I watched him struggle with the pancakes and preserves that Regina put out for us.

Regina wiped her hands on her apron and sat down between us.

"Shortly after the wedding, I went to Poldi's grandmother to say goodbye. The door creaked as I let myself in to the aroma of the herbs and the medicines she cooked there in her cottage. It was easy to feel ancient spirits hanging in the dark, close air. The people in town called the old one a drabarni, the gypsy word for fortune-teller, herb-dealer, healer. I visited her often, brought her treats, and told her about worlds she would never see. Those last months, she taught me how to pass hands, how to heal. She also told me Poldi's family history, and how it was now my responsibility to carry on the family name through sons.

"On that last day, I found the old one in her sleeping alcove. I bent down into the darkness to kiss her cheek. It was not the first time I saw the odd light around her head, the one that seemed to come from nowhere. With all my education I did not forget the sacred ways and the magic that must be respected and believed above all else. I lit the candle at the foot of her bed.

"'Grandmother, the air is filled with the perfume of spring.'

"'Eva, child, do not be fooled. That air will soon be filled with another smell.'"

"'Do you not remember? This is why we are leaving, why we have said goodbye to our friends, sold everything.'

"The grandmother sighed. She lifted herself onto her elbow.

"'There is one more thing,' she whispered. 'You are prepared. I have taught you the cures, the words, the chants. You will remember them always. Believe them. Teach them to your children.'

"She held out a small packet tied with faded, colorless ribbon. She looked up at me with eyes that glittered from the candlelight.

"I felt the ring before I finished opening the folded handkerchief. 'Oh grandmother, it is beautiful.'

"Tiny red jewels encrusted a raised gold center. 'It is not just a beautiful ring.' Her voice filled the cottage with a new force. 'There is something special in how it is made, see, here.' Her wrinkled hand moved toward my palm. Without looking she pushed her thumb against the side of the ring. The jeweled center sprang open like a locket revealing a brilliant diamond.

"'Oh Grandmother, I cannot take this.' My protest sounded feeble. 'I cannot take such a thing.' I slid the ring on my finger and slowly tilted my hand back and forth. The diamond winked blue at me as it caught the light from the candle.

"'You must take it.' The old one fell back on her bed. 'You have no choice. Without this ring you will have no sons.'"

Regina stopped talking. I didn't have to look at Rudy to know he was crying. So this was what he'd been talking about when he asked me to help him find the ring that first day. Only then he was laughing and I thought it was just a joke. I didn't believe him then and I didn't know if I believed this ring story now either.

"Rudy, tell her there is so much to think about. Tell her I will treasure the story." I smiled politely and said *spaciba*, thank you.

CHAPTER 13

Our second day in Chernovtsy was Rudy's birthday. It was also market day. Regina gave us straw baskets to carry and Rudy dragged out one of his five suitcases.

"What's with the suitcase?" I asked. "It's heavy."

"You'll see." Rudy placed it in the doorway leading out to the street. He stretched his arms high into the air. "Oh, what a day."

"Happy?"

"Happy isn't the word for it."

I took Rudy's arm. Regina took the other one. The word *Americansky* reverberated around us as people stared with open mouths. Their unbuttoned coats and the traditional fur hats pushed back from their foreheads made it suddenly feel like spring. Rudy chatted gaily with Regina as he navigated our threesome through the crowded street. I could tell he was making little jokes by how she blushed and slapped his arm. I didn't need to know what they were saying. The look on Rudy's face was enough. I wished someone could take a picture of us just then. The photograph would show the happiest people in the world plowing their way, arm-in-arm, through the Friday market crowd in Chernovtsy. Regina beamed at her neighbors, pointed to Rudy and winked.

Rudy leaned toward me. "You see how happy they are to see me? What a welcoming party."

"Yes. I see that."

"Now you know. This is my street. This is my home. These are my people."

I nodded. "Yes, I see that."

It was obvious that food was the first order of business in this city. "My goodness, Rudy, look. How many people are in that line? At least fifty." Two old women held faces up to the weak sun. Others read newspapers. Some gazed off into the distance.

"Funny thing is they don't even know what they are waiting for." We laughed as a woman wearing a rope of toilet paper rolls around her neck cut through the line.

"Well, judging from the laughter, they know what they are waiting for now."

"You think it's funny? You think not having toilet paper is funny?"

"I never thought about it."

"Newspaper." Rudy said. "That is what they use here. See those people in line? Do you think they bought the newspaper to read? There is nothing in that newspaper. They bought it for toilet paper."

"Really?"

"Really. Wait. You will see the nail, the squares of newspaper in the bathroom. Pink, perfumed toilet paper does not come with your orange juice here in the morning."

This time Rudy didn't sound angry.

The shouting, the smell of chickens and pigs hit me before
I actually saw the market. Boarded-up windows looked down
on the farmers' market in the courtyard of a crumbling church.
A cross etched into the cornerstone with Roman numerals
beneath it hinted this was once a place of worship.

I pulled on Rudy's sleeve. "It's a shame."

"What. Speak up, I can't hear you."

"I said it's a shame."

"What's a shame? It's great." Rudy rested the suitcase on the
ground. "Look around you. This is what it's all about."

"No, I mean it's a shame, the church and all."

"A church is for praying, no? So, here they are praying. Look,
see that old man there?"

An old man, his crutch leaning on the wall behind him, sat
cross-legged on a rug. In front of him, five eggs formed a line
in the dirt under a tiny canopy constructed of sticks. A red
kerchief shielded the eggs from the sun.

"He's praying, no? He's praying someone will buy his eggs.
A lot of praying going on here."

Next to me, a chicken peeked out from a peasant's basket.
A young woman with a baby on her back gazed proudly at her
pyramid of a dozen potatoes. A gypsy boy pressed a handful of
wildflowers into Rudy's face. Rudy gave him a coin and pushed
him back without taking the flowers.

A friend had saved a space for Regina in the middle of the
chaos. I closed my eyes for a second in thanks that it was not
hot. The noise and smells were enough.

Rudy put his suitcase down and pulled his shirtsleeves up.
Immediately people gathered around him. I realized they had
been following us.

"You are not going to open that here, now?"

"Of course I am. Why do you think I brought this heavy
suitcase? I told you. They have been waiting for me. These

people." Rudy stretched out his hand. "They knew I would come. Rudy always comes back."

"But are you allowed to do this?"

"What are you talking about? This is home. I can do what I want here." Rudy said something to Regina. They both looked at me and laughed.

"But what about police?"

"Look, it's market day. Friday. Market day. Nobody bothers us today." The group sighed in unison as Rudy opened the suitcase.

I stepped back into the crowd to watch him sell the jeans and pantyhose. As he took in the money he gave it to Regina, who dashed back and forth buying food. I saw that the process would not last long. As soon as Rudy picked up an item it was gone. Size and color were not important. I held up my hands and signaled to Rudy that I would be back in ten minutes. He smiled absentmindedly and waved goodbye.

I walked carefully up and down the narrow aisles of the market noting vendors and items that would guide me back to Rudy if I got confused. I bent to touch the hand of an old woman who was selling radishes and had reached out to touch my boot. The warmth from the sun penetrated my coat. I took a deep breath. I was no longer afraid of getting lost.

From the fringe of the market I crossed a boulevard and then dodged deep ruts in an unpaved side street. There were no street signs, no people. Once again, I felt I was in a dream as a haunting baritone voice drifted from an overhead window.

The cottage at the end of the road was secured with a rusty padlock. Warped shutters hung, half attached from the window frames. I ran my fingers over the Cyrillic letters on a tarnished plaque next to the door. I waited a few seconds before dropping my hand.

I stepped over a circle of herblike plants that pushed up

through the remaining snow and surrounded a stone bench. I sat down and took deep breaths of the pungent smell of plants struggling to survive in the late winter sun.

I closed my eyes. I didn't question why I was suddenly so tired. I was exactly where I was supposed to be, and it had been a long journey. I heard Rudy's voice that first day when he said he knew me. I heard his promise that he would take me home. And I remembered my promise to believe.

When I opened my eyes the sun was gone. An odd mist wound itself around my feet. I jumped up and ran back to the market where the last vendors were packing up. There was no trash or garbage anywhere to attest to what had transpired there. Rudy and Regina's space was empty.

"Where were you?" I turned to see Rudy behind me. "I thought you said ten minutes. I don't believe you."

"Sorry."

"No you're not sorry. Look at you. Smiling. And those rosy cheeks."

"Rudy, something magical just happened."

"Magical huh? It will be magical if we get back to Ivan Beguna before the snow starts."

"But there's a cottage down the road there. And it's just like you said. I had to believe everything."

Rudy picked up the empty suitcase. "But you forgot me."

"What are you talking about? Be serious. I understand. I finally understand."

"That's nice, but you did forget me, admit it."

I felt my old anger coming back for the first time since we left New York. "Why does everything have to be about you anyhow? You're like a damn child. Did I forget you? Did I forget you? So what if I did." I hit myself in the chest to impress him. "What if this is really all about me?"

Rudy took a few steps and looked down at the ground. "Well, at least I won't forget you."

"Hey, I'm up here." His wounded face cut right through my anger. "I guess now you'll give me some of those gypsy tears for good measure."

Rudy looked up and smiled. He grabbed my hand and gave me a harsh tug. "Damn gypsy, can't stay in one place, can you." His laughter echoed through the courtyard.

He pulled me down the street where blurred buildings whizzed by and the laughter of the people in Chernovtsy filled my heart.

CHAPTER 14

Haphazard snowflakes danced in the air that night as the guests arrived for Rudy's birthday party. I was on the swing outside, the one Beno put up for Rudy all those years ago. I watched the door, waiting to see if he would come looking for me, but I knew I was fooling myself. The door opened at each knock. Rudichka, Rudichka, the guests cried out as he hugged them all in the same rocking motion and kissed them loudly on both cheeks. My face was warm in the chill air from just seeing the smiles, the tears, the shine of gold teeth. I saw Regina through the kitchen window moving around quickly, pointing out directions to the two girls who helped her. Back and forth into the rooms they went, carrying platters piled high with stuffed potatoes. There was a whole fish. Steam rose from bowls of cabbage. The shadows of the guests, standing with their backs to the windows, converged on the snow-covered ground.

I sank my black velvet pumps into the snow and pushed

back, pulling on the ropes and lifting my feet. I threw my head back to catch the wet kisses of snow.

"Don't do that. Stop." Rudy's immense shadow spread out from the doorway.

"Why?" I raised my voice over the wind. "I'm having fun. This is great."

"You don't know how old those ropes are."

"Oh, yes, I do. As old as you, you old man you. Come push me, now!"

"If I push you," Rudy stuck out his chin, "will you come to my birthday party?"

"Yes, little boy. I will come to your party."

He walked toward me. His hips rotated just like they did on that first day I met him. Only now he was wearing the pants from his best pinstriped suit and the pale blue shirt with his initials embroidered on the pocket. His hair, in perfect order from an earlier visit to his old barber, was white with its light dusting of snow.

He stopped too close and I pulled my feet back just in time to avoid kicking him. He stood there with his hands on his hips for a few seconds, then took the cigarette out of his mouth and ground it into the snow.

"Come on, old man, push me."

"With my luck, the damn thing will break." Rudy walked behind the swing and gave me a powerful push. I flew up and returned for another push. His strength flowed through the swing and into my body as I reached a new height.

"Oh, this is wonderful!"

On the fourth push, Rudy caught the rope. "A deal's a deal." His voice was stern.

"Yes, okay." I wanted him to say something else. "Can you feel it?"

"Feel it?" he said.

"Yes, feel it." I knew from all the other times he wouldn't understand.

"You mean the magic?"

I gasped out loud. "You do understand."

"Yes, of course I understand. I understand everything. I may not show it but I understand, and I believe. And you think you know me." Rudy winked.

I looked up through the snowflakes sticking to my eyelashes. His face was serious as he took my hand and helped me off the swing.

The tinny sound of music came from an old portable phonograph set up in the corner of the living room. "Why is it so low?" I asked.

"Let's just say the neighbors around here don't appreciate Yiddish music."

"Oh. I forgot."

"It is easy to forget a lot of things. On a night like this it is okay to forget." Rudy leaned over and kissed me on the ear. "Except of course for you, Schveetheart. Do not forget me again."

"I won't forget you."

He led me around the room, introducing me to his guests. Although I did not understand what anyone said, I saw the admiration in their eyes. They loved him.

The men kissed my hand. The women's eyes moved from my head down to my velvet slippers and then back up again.

The weak music seemed appropriate for men dressed in 1940s-style double-breasted suits with wide ties. The women, mostly chubby and in thick nylon stockings and paisley rayon dresses, were obviously wearing their best.

An old couple helped each other to the middle of the floor. We watched their slow shuffling dance.

"Tears in your eyes again?" I loved to tease Rudy.

"No. Actually I may have had too much vodka."

"Hey! I'm supposed to say that."

"Excuse me. I am going to get Regina. I will be right back." Rudy walked toward the kitchen. A guest stopped him and pushed a glass into Rudy's hand. I could see by now it was an honor to drink with him. In a fluid movement Rudy threw the drink back, grimaced and moved on.

I motioned to Beno that I would like a drink. He hesitated as though wondering if I was old enough. I motioned again with my pinkie in the air the way Rudy did. Beno poured something into a delicate glass with gold rings around the rim. I filled my mouth with the clear, odorless liquid, attempting what I had seen Rudy do over and over with such ease and pleasure. I threw my head back and swallowed. Fire burned its way down my throat. I exhaled, expecting flames to shoot from my mouth as the blood rushed to my face. I reached out to grab Beno's arm. He called out for Rudy. Someone handed him a piece of dry bread. Rudy said I must eat it but my mouth did not work. He tore off a piece and coaxed me to open my mouth. I chewed the bread with tears streaming down my cheeks.

Rudy laughed. "Why did you do a crazy thing like that?"

"I, I . . ."

"You want to be like the rest of us?" Rudy stretched out his hand to the group that formed around us.

I nodded my head and kept chewing. The bread helped. I caught my breath and closed my eyes to stop the room from spinning.

"You can't be like us. Once an American, always an American. But it's okay. They like you anyhow. Actually they love you. You are the first American woman they have met, so you can't lose." Rudy stuck out his chest. "Besides you are with me."

"I'm sorry. It's just like you said. I want to be one of your people."

"It's okay, kid. Just sit there a while. And watch this." Rudy patted me on the shoulder, went back into the kitchen and came out seconds later pulling Regina behind him. Her face was flushed from the heat. Although she had a spotless white apron tied over her flowered housedress, the felt house slippers made it obvious she did not intend to come out yet. She pulled back but Rudy did not let go. Someone made the music louder.

It was slow music, the kind that holds the promise of getting faster. The old women formed a circle around Rudy. Their hands joined over each others' shoulders. In the center of the circle Rudy's head was thrown back. His legs were bent at the knee, and with arms outstretched, he snapped his fingers to the music. His feet did not move.

One by one the women came to the center to dance around him. The men shouting "Oppah, oppah" seemed to encourage the women to raise their shoulders suggestively. Rudy's eyes were closed.

I was fascinated by the sensual movements of these old women. Then it was Regina's turn. Rudy opened his eyes. He slid his arm over her apron so they were shoulder to shoulder, each facing the opposite way. She too had her arm outstretched across his body. They moved around and around slowly. Everyone shouted and clapped as the music quickened. Regina no longer shuffled in her flannel slippers.

"Oppah, oppah," was now a roar. Her feet barely touched the floor as Rudy spun her around. His free arm was raised high in the air. The sweat flew off his hair. His face was alive with a joy I had never seen.

The music stopped. Regina stepped back and hit Rudy on the arm. She tried to wipe his forehead with her apron but he caught her arm and twirled her around. Then he bent, clicked his heels, and lifted her hand to his lips as the guests cheered.

Rudy's wet shirt was stuck to his body. "You see? This is what we call a birthday."

"Yes, I see, I see."

Rudy looked back at the kitchen. "And my Tanta Regina?"

"Yes, I know. I'm so happy for you."

"Are you really?" He put his arms around me. "Are you really happy for me?"

"You deserve this, you know. You deserve this celebration. You have it coming to you."

"No. You got it all wrong. They have it coming to them."

"What do you mean? It's your party."

"But they need me. Don't you see that? They have been waiting for me for a long time."

"Yes, I guess that's one way to look at it."

"It is the only way."

The door to the kitchen opened. The voices faded. Regina carried a huge chocolate cake with a candle in the middle. One by one the guests lifted their glasses.

"What are they singing?"

"They are singing to my health, that I should live for a hundred years."

"I'll drink to that."

"Better hurry up." Rudy laughed as he raised his glass. "I'm almost there."

CHAPTER 15

According to regulations and our visa, we were supposed to sleep in the Buckovina, a government-owned hotel. At the end of the party Rudy looked out at the snow and decided we would stay where we were. I was worried we'd get into trouble but Rudy took out a roll of bills and reminded me that he had "enough money to buy the whole damn country."

In the middle of that night I wrapped myself in a blanket and tiptoed through the dark to find the bathroom.

Eight people slept in the rooms before me, including the cousins who insisted we take their room even though they had a new baby. They said Americans needed privacy.

I came back to the room when I realized I could not negotiate the obstacle course around the open couches and beds. "Rudy, wake up, please, wake up." I shook him. "I need you."

"What do you want now?" he mumbled from his vodka-induced stupor. "Where are you?" His warm hand brushed against my goose-bumped leg.

"Shhh, quiet, Rudy, you'll wake up everyone. I need to go to the bathroom. I can't see where to walk."

Rudy sat up in the narrow bed and scratched his chest. His naked body was a black silhouette against the streetlamp.

"Aren't you cold?" I asked.

"Cold? Why would I be cold? I was born here, remember? Right here in the middle of winter. And that night was much colder than this they tell me. Of course I'm not cold. So you have to go out?"

Going out was what Rudy called going to the bathroom. It had to do with being in the camps and literally having to go out into the woods to do what you had to do.

"I have to go bad, please, come on."

"Look, in this country you don't go out in the middle of the night. Next thing I know, you will want orange juice in the morning. Wait. Let me see something." He reached under the our bed. "Aha." He brought out a pot.

"Oh no. Tell me you're joking."

"No, I am not joking." He pushed the pot into my hands. I pushed it back.

"I want to go now." The hysteria in my voice must have convinced him. He grabbed his pants that hung on the bedpost and we tiptoed to the door. Rudy held my hand tight.

It was warmer in the next room. Little mewing sounds came from the baby fussing in his cradle. The only heat in the apartment came from the green-tiled heating device in the corner. In the next room older relatives slept with young grandchildren.

Beno and Regina slept in the kitchen on the bed I had wondered about when I arrived the day before. They were the most removed from the heat source. A light from the street glowed through the frosted window and fell on their bed.

Frigid air replaced the earlier food smells. In this austere room, beneath the feather bedding, Regina slept on with one arm holding Beno to her side. The faded pink of the featherbed softened the scene into a holiness. I stood there, my hand in Rudy's, watching them sleep as though a mighty hand had lifted a curtain and allowed us to peek. I stepped closer to see an open Hebrew prayer book. I imagined Beno leaning over his side of the bed, reading in the candlelight.

Rudy squeezed my hand and led me to the bathroom, where I made him stand guard at the door until I finished and poured the necessary pails of water into the bowl.

Back in bed we heated our frozen feet with the warmth of each other's body. In my sleep I felt Rudy move closer. I put my arm around him and held him to me.

In the morning we were in the same position. Sunlight streamed into our room.

Rudy lifted his head and kissed me on the cheek. "Don't worry. I heard you last night with those pails of water. You are one of us."

Chernovtsy, where Rudy smiled all the time and where he drank his vodka straight but never quite got drunk.

The morning after his party, Rudy led me down the streets where he played soccer when he was a child and explained again how he made schmataballs out of his mother's old stockings. We sat on a rock by the edge of the River Prut where he used to swim with the other boys. And then of course, I heard once more about the gypsies that camped there.

"Do you remember that day in Sinj?" I asked.

"Sinj?"

"Remember the gypsy woman on the street in Sinj that morning? You gave her all your money, remember?"

Rudy looked at me and winked. "Of course I remember. I never forget a gypsy girl."

"You know we never did finish that conversation in bed that day. When the wine was finished we just got up and left. I still remember the tune you whistled."

"This one?" Rudy whistled the same tune. He raised his eyebrows and deep lines appeared in his forehead.

"So, did they ever make you a gypsy? I remember they were getting ready to make you a gypsy."

Rudy stopped whistling.

"Good God, don't tell me they actually made you a gypsy."

Rudy didn't answer. He continued whistling as he laid back on the rock with his hands behind his head.

"Are you upset? I was only joking. I know people don't like being called gypsies. I know you can't just become a gypsy. Even I know that, right?"

"Wrong." His voice was flat.

"What do you mean wrong?"

"Wrong, as in wrong." Rudy removed one arm from behind his head and rested it in the space between us. "You have to understand. Gypsies believe you must be brother and sister before anything else."

"Don't talk to me like I'm a child."

"I know it was a little late, but we were children, re-member?"

"We? What do you mean we? Some children, you and that gypsy girl. And there's that blood-mixing thing, crossing wrists. It would be like you belonged to each other. Like forever."

"Perhaps, but you need to understand it was not what you say, ''til death do us part.' It's none of that. It was an oath we took. We would always be brother and sister, but one must leave the other as soon as love has left the heart. Love and freedom, remember the song? Not duty, not possession. Love and freedom."

I turned my head so Rudy wouldn't see my tear-filled eyes.

Rudy took my hand and brought it to that space between us.

"We belong to each other, don't we? We have always belonged to each other. You knew it that first day, when I looked at your hand and said I knew you. You agreed. You said yes. I told you to believe, remember?"

"Yes, but I didn't believe you would remember."

"Of course I remember." His thumb rubbed the inside of my wrist. "So then?"

"So then?" I echoed.

"So then look at your wrist."

"What? My wrist? You mean your wrist."

"No, I mean your wrist."

I was getting impatient. "Look, I don't understand."

Rudy's thumb stopped moving. "You will."

He lifted my hand before my face. It blocked the sun. Then he brought his wrist up next to mine.

He had the same small scar.

"My Grandma Bessie." My mind reeled with the recollection of how she once grabbed my hand and embedded her long red fingernails into my wrist.

"You mean that gypsy?" Rudy said.

CHAPTER 16

We stayed by the River Prut until purple shadows closed in around us. Once again there was little to say. Besides, too much was going on in my head. Rudy saw I was shivering and put his jacket over me. I wanted to tell him my chills had little to do with the falling temperature. I smiled and said thank you instead.

Rudy pulled me up once the sun had set behind the mountains. He brushed the leaves off my clothes. "So now you know," he said.

"Yes, now I know."

Rudy finished the story as we walked back to Ivan Beguna Street. He said he came back to the river one day and she was gone. Everything was gone except for the smoldering ashes.

"Soon after the Germans marched in, they cleaned out Chernovtsy, including us of course. Once we were in the camps I went to wherever there was gypsy music, and I listened to their stories. I whistled their songs to give me courage. I asked about her everywhere. Nobody knew anything of her or her people." Rudy shrugged. "Not that anyone would admit it if they did, not to a Gadjo boy."

On the way home from the river, I waited outside the Hotel Bukovina while Rudy went in and paid someone off to leave us alone. And so that night again we slept in the narrow bed in the back room on Ivan Beguna.

We slept on Regina's best embroidered linen. She insisted on it just like she insisted on washing my underwear and ironing it. The next morning I walked into the kitchen to find the women admiring the lace on my panties.

Rudy still had four suitcases bulging with the clothes he patiently collected and sorted over the previous year. He had washed the clothes and removed the wrappings and tickets so they wouldn't look new and be confiscated. On the fourth night of our trip, family and neighbors gathered to watch Rudy throw open one suitcase after another. Heavy sweaters, pantyhose, disposable cigarette lighters, lace bras, tee shirts with designer logos, and of course American jeans and boxes of Marlboro cigarettes tumbled onto the floor. I was uncomfortable as I felt the effort it took for these people not to pounce on the gifts. Rudy pretended to be oblivious to their awe. He took two big steps back, stretched his hands out modestly and apologized for such insignificant presents.

Our visas allowed us to stay in Chernovtsy for only five days. I left with a mind filled with unanswered questions and a pain in my heart that I did not comprehend or have time to explore. There was something there, something that set in motion an unexplainable longing. On the last day I brought up the issue of the ring. Rudy laughed and said this trip was only the beginning, and that we would come back soon.

A few minutes before midnight the Moscow-Sophia Express pulled into the station. As I watched them all hugging and crying goodbye, I hardly believed I would ever see them again.

CHAPTER 17

Beno's letter arrived only nine months after our first trip. Strangely, it was the same week Rudy had started talking about the ring again. The letter informed us Regina was dying.

The authorities in the Russian Embassy would not accept that we wanted to go back so soon. They wouldn't read Beno's letter. By the time our three-day visas were issued, Regina had been dead two months.

We arrived at the Chernatu station in an ice storm, with a wind that knocked Rudy sideways against the train. I knew that this time the border guards and their constant questioning had exhausted him. He hadn't slept since our arrival in Bucharest the day before. From my upper berth I watched him chain smoke all night, taking breaks only to throw his head back and swallow from the bottle under his berth. He had emptied his silver flask hours before.

I shielded my eyes and saw Beno on the platform under the

station lamp waving both arms. Rudy dropped our bags in the snow and jumped over the rails. Their moans mixed with the hiss of the train as they rocked in each others arms and cried out Regina, Regina.

It sounded like dying of cancer in a Russian hospital was a nightmare. The doctors and nurses were not attentive unless they were paid off, so the family took turns taking care of Regina. Beno never left her side. He brought basins of water to bathe her. He held her hand against his cheek and told stories recollecting their youth before the war. Regina kept asking for her Rudichka.

The first morning, from behind Regina's lace curtain I watched Beno pick his way over the icy street. His shoulders sagged under the weight of Rudy's heavy coat. The family told us he always left early for the cemetery while everyone was still asleep. They said it was useless to try to stop him. The night before, Beno had sat in the corner for hours and watched us with vacant eyes. Rudy attempted to talk to him but Beno's mind was in another place.

Now Rudy was behind me getting dressed. His hair stood straight up. He needed a shave.

"You're going like that?" I buttoned his shirt.

"I must catch up to him." His voice was hoarse. "He cannot go alone." Rudy started toward the door, hesitated, and rushed back to kiss me on the forehead. "It's too terrible," he said and was gone.

Back at the window I watched Rudy dash out through the gate. He slipped on the ice but caught himself on a tree. For a second I panicked but then quickly realized this couldn't happen. Rudy always said he knew how to live here, that this was his home.

On the second morning, I went with Rudy and Beno to the

Jewish cemetery. It was even more gray than the day before. We held onto each other as we worked our way down deserted streets. A brutal wind penetrated my coat. People with scarf-wrapped heads were outlined in the shadowy doorways of the old apartment buildings that were relics from the Austrian occupation. Somehow I hadn't noticed this decrepit scene on our first trip. I shuttered from both the cold and the sight of broken windows, the open garbage cans that filled the air with their smell, and the sinister hallways with crumbling, concrete steps.

I clutched Rudy's arm with both hands. His pale face was a mirror of the misery and emptiness around me.

Rudy brushed the snow off a wooden bench opposite the grave. We huddled there, with Regina peering out solemnly from the oval picture on her tombstone. The flowers in Rudy's limp hands hung between his knees. I didn't know what to do when he started to sob. I walked a few feet away and watched him and Beno rock in each others arms. I contemplated the dead flowers swirling about my feet and wondered how Rudy was going to survive this sadness. Beno said something and patted him on the back as Rudy walked to the edge of the grave. He knelt and gently put down the flowers.

When Rudy stood up and turned, he was an old man.

I struggled with Rudy's weight against me on our walk back to Ivan Beguna Street. An awful sadness settled in his shoulders, in the way he held his head. It dimmed the sparkle in his eye. We didn't discuss it on that trip but I knew that with Regina gone, Rudy thought his last hopes for the ring were gone too.

By the third day I couldn't help saying, "For God's sake, it's time to take responsibility for your life. Once and for all, stop being such a damn victim. The war is over."

Rudy looked at me. It was obvious he had no clue what I

was talking about. That was also the day he got the pain. He refused to see a doctor. He lit one cigarette with another and was always drunk to some degree. Rudy said he knew what the doctors would say. He said he was just tired. He was always tired.

CHAPTER 18

Back in New York, I tried. I failed. I tried again. Then came that one frigid evening when I decided not to go back into the bunker. In my car with the motor running, I waited for Rudy to come home from work. The street was empty. I watched the snowflakes fall in the light of the streetlamp and kept repeating to myself, I'm okay, I'm okay. It's time to give up. I had to keep reminding myself that life in the bunker after our return from our second trip to Chernovtsy was a bad dream.

Most nights Rudy came home later and later, first midnight, then one, then two o'clock in the morning. It was the gambling. After Regina's death, as he skidded from one drunken depression to the next, he started to talk about the thousands of dollars he was losing. He also admitted that he'd gambled all the time we'd been together, and way before that as well. Atlantic City, and then the race track caught hold after years of secretly dashing in and out of off-track-betting storefronts.

I waited for those brief periods when he was really broke, to talk to him. When there was no more "shit money" he was able to listen. Mornings were best with that one shaft of light coming through the little window over our bed.

"See how the light comes in and rests on your heart?" I tapped Rudy's chest.

"I thought you said I had no heart. Remember, you said I had no heart."

"It's hard to remember you have a heart when you do what you're doing to us."

Rudy looked over with eyebrows raised in amazement. "To us? What do you mean to us?"

"To us, to us. What do you think your way of life is doing to us?"

"Look kid. I know I'm wrong, okay? But I'm doing it to myself, not you. I'm only hurting myself."

"Okay, so you're only hurting yourself. If you want to believe that, okay. But why? Why do you have to destroy yourself like this? Look at you. Look how skinny you're getting. You're wasting away. Nothing you eat makes a difference. It's the nicotine and the alcohol poisoning your body." My voice was too loud. "You think I don't know you spend your money on horses instead of food. You think I don't know?"

"You don't know. I am trying to survive."

"Survive? You must be kidding. You call this surviving? I don't believe that's what you call it. Explain it to me."

"You're getting hysterical. Besides, it's a long story."

"I have time."

"Well, I don't have time. Look, it's six-thirty already. I have to get up."

"No you don't. You can wait five more minutes. Here, stay with me. Put your head here. Talk to me. Just talk to me, for

God's sake. Tell me why. Why do I call it destroying and you call it surviving?"

Rudy rested his head on my shoulder. "Pain." he said. "It's a long story. It is about pain."

"But what about the pain the day after? Doesn't that hurt?" I tried to control myself but the pitch of my voice got higher. "Isn't that bad enough? And what about my pain? I have to watch you."

Rudy's body was tense. "Look, I have to go. I have a lot to do. We'll talk tonight. I promise." Rudy lifted his head and tried to pull away.

"Stop running. For God's sake stop running. You don't have to run anymore. It's over. It's all over. You can rest now. Rest with me, I'll show you how." I let go.

Rudy swung his legs over the side of the bed and sat up. "You don't understand. It's not over. I have to clean myself out, finish the job."

Most nights I came home from work and rushed down the driveway, straining to see if the lights were on. I almost always walked down the two steps into an empty bunker. I'd turn on the electric heater next to our bed, make a cup of tea on the hot plate, and wait. There was no window I could look out of to watch for Rudy, so I listened to cars passing in the street, hoping to hear his broken muffler. Leaves rustled in the driveway and my heart jumped. Finally when my eyes got heavy I went to our bed. Still wearing my clothes, I rolled up in the blankets. I smelled his cold pillow, rested my head there and waited.

One night, at about two o'clock in the morning the door crashed open as far as it would go with the chain on it. "Open the damn door," Rudy shouted.

I didn't answer. I went to the door, shut it and slid the chain off. I turned quickly before the door opened. "Schveetheart, aren't you going to say hello?"

The bunker filled instantly with the smell of alcohol. I got back into bed and turned to the wall.

"Okay, okay, so I'm a little late." Rudy banged his fist against the wall. "What's the big deal?" He pulled his jacket off, lost his balance and fell against the dresser.

The blood rushed to my face. "Son of a bitch."

"What, what did you say?"

"Nothing."

He went into the bathroom. I heard him use the toilet but he didn't flush. He didn't turn on the water in the sink either. The bathroom door crashed open.

I tried to control my voice. "Go back and flush the damn toilet."

"I did."

"I said go back and flush the damn toilet. And try washing your hands this time, you son of a bitch."

"Lay off. I'm tired."

"Don't you dare come near this bed."

"Okay, okay." Rudy walked back to the bathroom and flushed the toilet. He turned the water on in the sink. In one second it was off again.

He stood over me.

"Don't you dare."

"Hey, wait a minute. See, I washed my hands."

"You call that washing your hands? You stink. Go sleep on the floor for all I care. Get away from me."

He moved closer. I put my foot out to hold him back but he grabbed it and pushed it away. "Take it easy kid, trying to kick me huh?"

Rudy turned and went to the far corner of the bunker where

I had set up an old foam beach mat with a sheet, a blanket and a pillow. This was not the first time he was sleeping there. In a minute he was snoring.

Four hours later he stood in the dim morning light, putting on the same clothes. He banged into the bathroom and out again.

I held my breath as he walked to the door. He hesitated for a moment as though he had forgotten something. Then he slammed the door behind him.

I got up and went to the corner. I stooped down and got under the cover that was still warm from his body. "Son of a bitch," I cried out loud. "Lousy son of a bitch."

Before I left for work that morning I fixed his bed. I felt foolish but I did it anyhow. I changed the sheet, smoothed out the wrinkles and turned the blanket down.

I'd been sitting in the car for an hour when Rudy appeared out of the dark. I come from nowhere, he once said. Nobody wants me. His head was down. I blinked my headlights and he saw me. He opened the door and jumped in.

"What's up, kid? Can't find a parking space?" He rubbed his red hands in front of the heater vent.

"No, that's not it."

"Well come on then, park the car and let's go in."

"I can't."

"Why not, look there's a space."

"I can't."

Rudy reached up and flicked on the overhead light. "Hey, what's the matter? Why are you crying?"

"Look Rudy, I can't. I can't come into the bunker."

"I don't understand."

I saw that he really didn't understand. "I can't come into the bunker, not ever again."

Rudy's eyes opened wide. "I, I don't understand. What happened?"

"I've had it. I can't take it anymore. I love you, you know that. You knew it before I did. I just can't. I'm tired, too tired. I need to get some sleep. I need to be alone. I don't know, I can't go down into that bunker with you." I waited. I looked down. His shoes were wet.

"Look, I know these last months have been rough. I need some time to pull myself together, that's all. Give me some time." Rudy smiled his little-boy smile. "And what about loyalty?"

"I've given you time. I've been loyal. It hasn't worked. I can't watch what you're doing to yourself. Don't you understand?"

"No." Rudy's hand rested on the door handle. "The gypsy says love means absolute loyalty."

I wanted him to grab me, grab my wrist, drag me out of the car. I wanted him to get angry. Tell me you hate me, I thought. Tell me you will change. Lie to me, say something.

Rudy leaned over and pressed warm lips against my cheek. I swallowed a sob when he opened the door. A cold wind rushed into the car and knocked him back. He said, "So, I'll call you tomorrow and we will work something out." Rudy disappeared into the dark, into nowhere. I shifted into drive and stepped on the gas.

I stayed at a motel those first few nights. The next afternoon I went back into the bunker one more time to get my things. I saw that he had slept on the mat even though I wasn't there.

CHAPTER 19

An old couple who were once my parents' friends rented me a room overlooking the sound in City Island. They were on their way to Florida for the winter and I was to watch their house for them, so the rent was cheap. The first few nights we'd have a cup of tea together and talk about my family and what they remembered. My father had died years before, and mother shortly after I met Rudy. The old man retold my father's fishing stories. The woman remembered how devoted my mother was. I could almost feel my mother and father with me. City Island was a good place for me to be.

Even though I was not far away from Rudy distance-wise, that I was on an island seemed to help me separate and think, sometimes. The old couple had never met Rudy but they didn't ask about what I had been doing recently and I welcomed their good manners.

I woke on dark winter mornings to the laughter of the old fishermen on the pier. The sound of their spinning reels comforted me as I remembered how my father, too, fished well into the winter. I'd pull on a sweat suit and run downstairs to the luncheonette next door. Then I'd stand out on the pier, sipping my hot coffee and listening to the old men while the sun came up. Their tanned wrinkled faces eyed me suspiciously at first. Colorful checkered flannel shirts peeked out from their jackets. I wondered if they each wore two, like my father had. Their pants were baggy and stained. It didn't take long to feel my father's presence on those mornings too. He was right there waiting for the real catch after the eels left. The men of the island, the strong winds, and the rosy shimmer on the sound as the sun came up brought me back to life.

In my room I'd dress for work and throw open the window for one last deep breath. I'd exhale and sigh, "Rudy," hoping the wind would carry his name to wherever he was.

The City Island Bridge, outside my window, connected the island with the mainland. I was a twenty-minute drive from the bunker. I watched for Rudy. Sometimes I thought I saw his old blue Datsun crossing the bridge but it was only a little game I played because I knew it would never happen. Rudy knew where I was. All I wanted was to look out one morning and see him downstairs, sitting in his car, looking up at my window. I would run downstairs and he would ask me to walk with him down City Island Avenue. He would hold my hand tight the way he always did. I did invite him once, over the phone, to stop by some morning to go for a walk. "Not my style," he said.

After a few weeks, it took a lot of coffee and wind to keep me awake most mornings because of my craziness the night before. I'd sit in my car down the block from the bunker with my lights off and watch for him. I knew he came home early when he was broke. He'd appear out of the dark and quickly disappear down the driveway. At least I knew he was home.

Other nights he did not appear. I had to turn my motor off

because I was afraid I'd fall asleep and not wake up. My feet froze. Gloves didn't help. At ten o'clock, I'd strain to see down the dark street to the corner. I told myself, five more minutes, just wait five more minutes. Finally I'd start the engine and drive back to my room, where terrifying loneliness waited. I needed Rudy. But I needed him to need me, too.

I went to three recovery meetings for family and friends of compulsive gamblers. I went to Alcoholics Anonymous meetings. I met caring, nurturing people who hugged me and assured me that I must keep coming back. I did not have the courage to tell them Rudy was of a different breed. The camps, the ring, the family in Chernovtsy, the son he never had were too much for him. I quit going to meetings.

In the beginning I called Rudy every morning at his shop when I got to work. One morning no one answered. I called him that night in the bunker but I knew that was a waste of time. I set my alarm and called him in the bunker at five-thirty the next morning. The phone just rang.

After a week of attempts I finally got Rudy on the phone. He laughed as he told me about how he'd just spent a week in jail for drunk driving. He had also lost his license for ninety days. He wasn't laughing about the engine in the Datsun burning out for lack of oil. Rudy was taking a bus and then a subway to his shop in Brooklyn.

Our telephone exchanges were brief. Rudy had never liked talking on the phone but now he'd always finish our conversations by saying, "I won't forget you." The pain of hearing his voice was almost more than I could bear.

The paralyzing February blizzard came without warning. There was no electricity or phone service anywhere in the city.

I knew Rudy was in the bunker and saw him lying on the beach mat in the dark cold corner. Son of a bitch, I repeated as I paced back and forth in front of my window. The snow drifts piled higher and higher. The water around the island iced over and the buoy bells were silent. I contemplated the frozen surface of the bridge that connected me with Rudy.

I stayed up as late as I could that night because I knew what the dreams would be like. Whenever I was vulnerable, or angry with him I'd have the same painful dream. Rudy and his peasant women were always waiting to taunt me.

Rudy had a way of speaking to peasant women in their language, and in that deep and teasing voice he saved. He slipped into another language so easily, so intimately, it was as though he'd actually slipped into the peasant woman herself.

There was that sunny afternoon in Romania when Rudy sat next to such a woman who was selling blueberries. I watched him from across a narrow road where I was supposed to be buying vegetables. Rudy stretched his arm along the back of her bench, crossed his legs and leaned back, watching her through narrowed eyes. She bent to the ground, took a handful of berries from her basket and gave them to him. The way Rudy rolled them around in his hand made me think of diamonds. He popped them one at a time into his mouth. I tried not to look when he held out his hand for more.

It was those times, when I was sure he forgot me, that I hated him the most.

So it was in City Island. In my despair, one of these women kept coming back to me in my dreams. She was no fantasy. She was the sturdy, buxom peasant on the Sophia-Moscow Express on our second trip to Chernovtsy. Rudy was almost always drunk on that trip. He'd hardly slept once we got to Bucharest. He seemed anxious to drink with anyone he could find.

The train rocked gently through the snow-covered hills of Romania. Rudy sat on his lower berth, his knees almost touching those of a peasant woman opposite him. Her eyes fixed on his flask. He looked up at me for a second and said he was going to practice his Romanian. I curled up in the corner of the sleeper and tried not to watch the almost invisible space between their knees. Often the train took an unexpected lurch and his knees did brush hers. My nausea centered first around their knees but then moved to their conversation, which blocked me out of Rudy's world, their world. The peasant woman's huge breasts hung to her stomach. Her arms were covered with long woolen sleeves that stretched to the seams. The strong smell of garlic mixed with that of her body.

Finally the flask was empty and crushed paper cups littered the floor. The woman was gone and Rudy was snoring in his berth. I wondered what might have happened had I not been there.

In my recurring dream I saw that peasant woman. I saw her on top of him. Her huge buttocks spilled over his slim hips. Rudy gazed up at her through heavy lids. He raised his hands as if to grab her, but then let them drop. His fists closed around the rumpled sheets under him.

She lifted herself on powerful arms and then came down with all her weight and spread her great thighs even more. The taunt muscles in her arms tightened as she locked him inside her. Her pendulous breasts swayed before him as his eyes followed the stretched nipples. I heard her wetness, and each time, before her body swallowed him, I saw the juice between their bodies.

An agonizing sound came from Rudy's open mouth. His lips quivered as drops of sweat fell from her breasts onto his face. His head lifted slowly from the pillow while his hands still clutched the sheets. Her brown nipples hardened and moved faster as his head rose higher. He didn't touch her. His body twitched. She put her hands on his shoulders and mumbled something in another language. She held him down firmly and stopped moving.

"Yes," he cried. "Yes." She bent closer and let the nipple fall near his mouth. Suddenly, his body shot up as the nipple disappeared into his mouth and they cried out together.

CHAPTER 20

The next morning I woke to bright sunlight. Melting snow dripped from the gutters and cars crunched down City Island Avenue. I lay in bed and thought about what the day might bring. I saw myself walking into the bunker, calling out Rudy's name. I'd bend to the bed mat and gape into Rudy's blue face.

Cars skidded across the bridge. Their tires whined but they moved. I put on most of the winter clothes I had and went out into the crisp air. Icicles shimmering on the trees made tiny tinkling sounds that reminded me of Mountain Lodge and how long it had been since we'd been there.

"Need some help, kid?" My heart skipped a beat. I looked up at the smiling face of the old fisherman. Two of his cronies lingered behind him.

"I don't think so. Oh, yes, I mean yes, I do. Thank you."

The men brushed off the car. "A nice-looking woman like

you should have a gentlemen friend to help." He laughed and winked. "Up there in that room, still in bed, is he?"

"No." My face got hot.

"Well, you been hanging out six o'clock in the morning with a bunch of smelly old fisherman all this time. Must be something wrong somewhere."

I laughed. "It's just that he travels a lot, international business and all. We have a place upstate. We see each other most weekends. It's okay, really."

The smiling fisherman took off his mittens and slapped the snow against his thigh. "Damn shame," he said seriously. The way he looked at me made me a little girl again.

"Gee, thanks a lot. Great job. I better get going."

"Going? Where you going? It's too icy up there on the bridge. Can't you see all that slipping and sliding? One of them's going to slide right into the sound. You watch and see."

"I'll be all right. I have to go. Someone needs me."

"Not going to be able to help anyone if you go over the side. Come on with us to the diner for a hot chocolate. Girl like you probably drinks hot chocolate."

"It's okay." I backed up toward the car.

The old man reached out and touched the sleeve of my jacket with his dark wrinkled hand. "Not going to be the end of the world if you have a hot chocolate with an old man, you know. Not like someone's going to die or something like that, is it?"

"Well, actually my friend's in trouble. She lives on the street." I looked out over the frozen sound to avoid his eyes. "I have to go find her."

"They got places for folks like that. You know that, don't you? Your friend's probably nice and cozy on some cot in a shelter. City's big on shelters this year."

"Not this friend. She's sort of proud."

"Can't imagine anyone being too proud to take a little warmth and soup on a day like this. Or even a little hot chocolate. What do you say?"

I hesitated and tried not to look at the bridge. I didn't have to look. I heard the cars trying to get across. I nodded and trudged along behind the men down City Island Avenue.

We sat around the table. Harry, the one who convinced me to come, sat opposite me. They were talking about the size of the last fish they caught that season and how long the water would stay frozen. Harry watched my face but didn't say a word. I sipped my cup of chocolate and studied how the frozen water glistened through the spaces between the houses on the avenue. I felt like he was waiting for me to say something.

I never did tell him my name. Somehow I didn't think it was important. That he called me kid was enough. He waited silently until I finished my hot chocolate. He tipped his hat when I said goodbye.

Back at the car I let the engine idle until it was warmed up. A sanding truck rolling over the bridge and back again seemed like a gift just for me. I waved at the driver and realized it was good I'd been delayed with that hot chocolate.

It took me an hour to do the twenty-minute ride. Snowed-in cars filled all the spaces on Rudy's block. I parked illegally, left my blinkers on and walked carefully through the knee-deep snow to the bunker. I knocked on the door.

"Rudy? Rudy are you there? It's me." I clutched the old key in my coat pocket. It seemed like years since I swore I'd never go into the bunker again.

I put the key in the lock with a shaky hand and turned. The chain was not on and the door swung open with a crash against the wall.

I stood in the doorway and called into the dark basement. "Rudy?" I stepped down. It was colder in the bunker than it was outside.

He was covered with a pile of blankets and clothes on the beach mat. The heater hummed but there was no red glow. The elements were burned out. Still blinded by the snow, it was difficult to see him. "Rudy, it's me."

Rudy's head moved. I bent down. His hand slid out from under the covers. He took my hand and brought it to his lips. "Schveetheart, you've come back to me."

"Where else would I be on a day like this? My God, what are you doing here?"

"Hygranating. I'm hygranating."

"Hygranating?"

"Yes, hygranating, don't you know what hygranating is?"

"Oh, hybernating, you son of a bitch. Still working on your English, huh?"

We laughed until I couldn't breathe.

"You look cold. Poor kid, come on under here." Rudy held up the mountain of blankets.

"You must be kidding. Tell me you're kidding."

"I am not. Look, look how warm it is." Rudy pulled my mitten off and placed my hand in the space under his body.

"I, I don't think so." I tried to pull my hand away, but he wouldn't let go. I slid into Rudy's warmth. Then he tucked the ends of the blanket around me like he always did.

CHAPTER 21

There was still Mountain Lodge, empty, waiting. After the blizzard and whenever I felt Rudy had pulled himself together enough, I'd pick him up. I had a mental list of criteria he had to meet before he could be with me. He had to be shaven, his hands and his clothes had to be clean. He had to be sober. He was not allowed to use the phone to check on his bets, and he had to split the bills for gas, food and the Sunday papers.

I knew it was ridiculous, but every Friday night I'd evaluate him in my car outside the bunker.

"You are without mercy." Laughter sparkled in his eyes again.

"Self-protection, it's called. You taught me that too, remember?"

"I was talking about the camps. Not this."

I could see Rudy was thoroughly enjoying our exchange. "You think it's a game. Look at you. Forget it. I'm going up alone. You haven't even tried."

"What is it this time? Tell me, I'll go inside and fix it."

I detested going up to Mountain Lodge alone, and he knew it. With Rudy along I sat in the warm car until he started a fire. I never left him behind.

One night my Jeep struggled up the mountain, skidding and sliding in and out of snowdrifts. Halfway up Rudy got out with the shovel to dig out the back tire. He paused before getting back in and looked up at the sky. "No stars tonight, going to get snowed-in tomorrow."

"It's okay with me," I said. Rudy didn't know how true that was.

Once in the cottage, it took him a few minutes to start the fire. He returned to the Jeep with one of his most magnificent smiles. "It's safe, you can come out now."

"What's with the smile? Don't you know you are not supposed to smile anymore? You said it is against your new religion, remember?"

"You're cute. Do you know you're cute? Does your mother have any more home like you?" Rudy opened my door and pulled me out. I fell against him. "See how you need me."

Once we made it up to the cabin, everything was like it used to be. I realized that the weeks he'd had big gambling losses were the weeks he took great pride in doing little things around the cottage. He mumbled when he brought in the wood to keep the fire going. He mumbled about being taken advantage of. But while he complained, he made me huge breakfasts or covered me up in the rocking chair until the cottage warmed up. He brought me tea in a little pot. I didn't say anything. He was struggling to be useful, to do something right. I was ready to cry almost all the time.

One night I sat in front of the fire, pretending to read but watching our shadows on the wall. Rudy crouched in the red wooden children's chair I'd bought for no reason. He looked up with empty eyes and sighed, his thin lips almost nonexistent. There was nothing to say.

"You need a drink, don't you?" I asked.

"You might say that. But you, you won't let a guy live."

"That's not what living is."

"Let's drop it. I didn't complain, did I? Besides, you like to see me suffer. Admit it, you like to see me suffer."

"How can you say that? Don't you know by now? I'm trying to save you. Don't you know that?"

"Do me a favor. Don't save me. Let me be happy. Let me live my way."

"I never said you couldn't live your way. I said you couldn't live your way and live with me. How many times do I have to tell you?"

"I'm going to sleep. We're running low. I have to chop some more wood in the morning." Rudy walked halfway to the bedroom and stopped. He didn't turn around. "By the way, what are you saving me for?"

"What do you mean, what am I saving you for?"

"Just what I said. What in hell are you saving me for?"

"That's a dumb question if I ever heard one."

"So give me a dumb answer."

"Go to sleep. Will you please just go to sleep."

I heard Rudy tossing around in bed. I thought about all the people who would look in on our scene with envy, the crackling fire, the snow-covered branches brushing against the little windows, the warm pine-scented air. Outside, our lantern cast soft light over the blue-white snow.

Save me for what, he asked. What was I saving him for? I couldn't think of an answer. Maybe I was just tired. I did know there was a longing deep inside me that kept us together. And it was because of that longing that I needed to keep Rudy alive.

I put a log on the fire and stopped at the bedroom door to listen to his breathing. I considered sleeping on the couch. What did I want? My clenched fists were tight against my sides. It shouldn't be like this, I thought. I deserved better. He deserved better.

"Schveetheart, aren't you coming to bed? I need you."

"You what?"

"I need you. Is that a crime? I always need you. I just don't talk about it much."

"You never said that to me before."

"So? Come to bed."

"Just like that?"

"Just like that."

I stood at the foot of the bed where I knew he could see me in the moonlight. I took off my robe. The cold air brought me back to the kitchen where Beno and Regina slept that night in Chernovtsy. The air had the same pure smell. I walked to Rudy's side of the bed. He reached up and caressed my thigh.

"You are shivering," he said. My skin tingled from his touch and his hushed voice.

"I'm just cold. Rudy, can we pretend this is the first time?"

Rudy took my hand and pulled me toward him. "Anything you want."

"I want so much to stay here, just like this, forever."

His warm lips move up my thigh. "Like this?"

Afterward, we heard snow crunch outside. "It is a deer!" Rudy propped himself up to look out the window over our heads.

"Maybe not. Maybe someone is sneaking up on us."

Rudy laughed the way he laughed only after making love. He pulled me close and moved the lace curtain aside. Then he blew warm breath on the frosted window and wiped a round spot for us to look through.

"Look, it is a deer." Rudy's voice was filled with an excitement that made him into a child again.

I looked out. "I don't see anything."

"Well, do you see it now? You see it, don't you?"

I made out the shape of a small deer. I turned toward Rudy and our checks touched. I looked into his eyes. He didn't look away like he usually did.

"So?" I asked.

"So?"

"So you said you need me."

"Yes, I know."

"What do you need me for? Tell me. Just this once. I promise you will still be alive after you tell me. Admit it just once, and see if you crumble up and die."

I felt him weighing what I said. I waited a few seconds and fell back on my pillow. I turned toward the wall.

"He can't go on alone." Rudy's serious voice shocked me.

"Who?" I asked as though I didn't know.

"That little deer out there. He's scared, weak. He can't keep running. He's tired. Most of all, he can't handle the freedom. He never could." Rudy's voice cracked. "I need you because I need to be obligated."

"Obligated."

"Yes, obligated. I need to know you are waiting for me, that someone waits for me. As long as I know you are waiting, I have to survive. I have to come back."

I wanted to remind Rudy of all the weeks before I moved and when he was out of control. He was obligated then, and he knew I was waiting. I didn't say a word. That Rudy was making this speech was enough.

He lay down beside me and pulled me close. His head was heavy, heavier than I remembered. It hurt my breast, but I didn't move.

I felt his wet cheek and tasted his tears on my hand.

"Save me then. You said you want to save me."

Rudy's suffering was a suffocating presence in the room. It was one thing to try and save Rudy when he didn't want to be saved. His sober tears did not feel good now. I was back in the bunker on those nights when I yelled, screamed at him. He was the one who was in control then. I was the one who needed him. All that noise to cover up the truth.

Rudy was asleep. His face was soft and young in the moonlight. I bent over to inhale his warm breath.

"Rudy?"

"Mmmmm . . ."

"Where are you?"

"Home."

"Do you want to go home?"

"Yes, I have to go home. They are waiting for me. I must go back."

"Then we will go back."

CHAPTER 22

Rudy was alive again. On the nights I waited for him outside the bunker, my heart pounded with the old excitement. We rode up to Mountain Lodge with Rudy whistling sweetly to gypsy music on the tape player. His walk was back. I watched him park his new car and rush down the street using those calculated, hip-grinding steps I loved. I was sure he could spring up off the pavement if he wanted to.

My car door flew open. He popped his head in and kissed me hard on the cheek. The overhead light sparkled in his eyes. "Here's more for the kitty." He threw a fistful of money into my lap. It was only a month and already he had accumulated enough money for the trip home.

I sorted the tens and twenties, making neat bundles in my lap. "Wow, look at this. Where did it come from?"

"You know. A chicken here, a chicken there."

"Cute, real cute. Does your mother have another one like you?"

"Hey, that's my line." His loud voice made the people on the street look at us.

"They're looking at us again," I said.

"Yes, isn't it wonderful?"

"Right. Let's get going."

"Wait, open the back." Rudy dashed over to his car trunk and pulled out a huge brown suitcase. He stopped for a breath halfway between his car and mine from the weight of it.

"Another suitcase?"

"Clothes for Beno. New clothes."

"Fell off the back of a truck again, I suppose."

"Why do you always think of me as a goniff? I happen to be an honest boychik."

"Yeah, I remember. So what kind of clothes?"

"Everything. Some are too big for him, but he will sell what he can't use. A warm jacket. It's blue and filled with feathers and has all those zippers. He will love it."

Rudy moved fast when he was happy. His eyes darted about checking out everything at once. In a whirl of excitement he had reserved our plane tickets and dictated an airmail letter to send to Beno. Our visas came through with unusual speed.

It was three days before our departure. We still had no answer from Beno. Rudy said it didn't matter. We were going home. There were two small suitcases for us. The five for Beno were immense. Almost every night after work Rudy went to the Laundromat to wash the new clothes so he wouldn't have trouble at the border. He tore the labels off the colorful dresses, sweaters and shirts. He bought a gentle baby detergent for Beno's blue jacket. He tucked batteries, aspirin, hair ribbons into shoes and boots.

Most evenings while he did the laundry, I sat in the car and read my paper. One night I glanced through the Laundromat window and saw Rudy's hands flying in the air. I knew he was

telling one more person his story about going home. A cigarette dangled from the corner of his mouth as he held up a
dress just out of the dryer.

Rudy, I wanted to call out. He doesn't care. Don't you know
that by now? I sighed and went back to my paper.

Rudy bounced into the car. He threw the bags of finished
laundry in the back seat.

"He didn't care," I said.

"Huh, what?"

"The guy, that guy you were just talking to. He didn't care."

"Don't you think I know that?" Rudy's angry voice startled
me. "I always knew that. Nobody cared then either."

This third trip was different from the others. Ukraine was
fighting for its independence from Russia. Chernovtsy, part
of the province of Bukovina, was going to become a city in
Ukraine. It was apparent though, as soon as we boarded the
train in Bucharest, that Russia was making life difficult for
those trying to break away.

The unheated empty train crawled with roaches. Rudy
complained to an old conductor in the corridor while I dozed,
my chin buried deep in my fur collar. When he came back
to report what he'd just heard, his body filled the doorway of
our compartment. The lights had not yet been turned on, so I
couldn't see his face.

"There is no money."

"No money. What do you mean, no money?"

"The conductor makes twelve dollars a month if he gets
paid at all. He hasn't been paid for three months. The people
do not have money to ride the train."

"What about the restaurant car?"

"You must be kidding."

"Why are you laughing? We have no food. We have nothing
to drink. It's cold. And the romance? Where's the romance?"

"It is only thirteen hours. You can take it. We took it."

"Sure, what do you care? You have your bottle."

"You want some?" He winked. "It will warm you up."

"No way."

"You will change your mind."

Two hours later I took a sip of brandy from Rudy's flask.

Its warmth spread quickly through my veins. I thought about the other trips, how they had seemed so elegant. Perhaps I had imagined it. In any case the elegance was gone.

I tucked my clothes in as best I could but soon felt a roach crawl up my leg. I squealed, "A roach" and jumped up.

Rudy was in the corridor watching the passing towns. He didn't turn around. "Sorry Schveetheart," he said over his shoulder and went on smoking.

I decided not to complain for the rest of the trip, even though the urine smell from the bathroom was nauseating. It was just as well we had no food.

I opened my suitcase. "Here, put on this sweater."

"I'm not cold."

"How can you say that? Let me feel your hands."

"I said I'm okay."

"Rudy, please." I grabbed his hand. "It's ice cold, what's the matter with you?"

"Nothing is the matter. You have to get used to these things. By the way, I may as well tell you. They say it's bad in Chernovtsy."

"You mean those things in the newspaper were true? Those things you said were propaganda?"

"Yes, I guess so. There is no heat anywhere in the city. The water is turned off most of the time, and when it is turned on, it is cold. No hot water."

"It's okay. I will heat the water."

"Right, the electricity is off most of the time too."

The fear in my stomach had been there, waiting. "It's okay. I can manage."

"I'm sorry. What can I say?"

"What should you be sorry for? It's not your fault."

"It is my fault." Rudy reached up and squashed a giant roach on the wall with the back of his cigarette pack. "Everything is my fault. Don't you know that by now? Everything."

He sat down and put his arm around me, pulling me back into the berth. We stayed huddled like that with Rudy humming the mysterious song with no melody. I didn't think about my cold feet or the urine smell. Rudy covered my two hands with his one hand. He buried his face in my hair and took a deep breath.

As we approached Chernovtsy the weather changed. Only hours before they had taken him off the train once again for the border inspection in a howling snowstorm. Now, except for gray patches of snow lining the tracks, there was no hint of winter. A sweet breeze caressed my face when Rudy opened the window in our compartment. He was very sober and still in shock that the border guards had let him through without a problem. This time they only took him off the train. I paced back and forth, ending each time in the open space between the cars where I strained to see him in the station window. Barely thirty minutes had passed when I heard him call my name. I rushed to the opening as the train's hissing turned into a powerful roar. Rudy ran toward me through the snow, his coat flying out around him, just like that last time.

I never found out what he said to them, or how they let him go so quickly. He said it was a long story.

The train pulled into the station in the afternoon, right on time. Rudy sighed in relief, but at the same time, his hand suddenly shot up to his chest.

"What's the matter?"

"Nothing." He pulled out his handkerchief and wiped his upper lip. "It's just the excitement. You know." He looked away.

The train screeched to a halt. Rudy pulled the suitcases from the overhead racks and slid them down the long corridor to the end of the car. He pushed me away when I tried to help. Tiny beads of sweat dotted his forehead as he struggled alone. He held out his hand and helped me down from the train, clicking his heels like those other times. "Welcome home," he said.

One by one, Rudy bumped the heavy suitcases down the steps and then over the tracks to the platform. I looked around for a porter out of habit, but I knew from the other times there was no one to help. For a second, Rudy let go of a suitcase. His hand rose up to his chest but only for a second. He saw I was watching so he dropped his hand to his breast pocket and fumbled with a pack of cigarettes.

Beno was not under the lamppost where he'd been the other times. Somehow, despite the bustling crowd in the station, I knew instantly he wasn't there. Rudy scratched his head.

"I don't understand it. Beno is always here." The smile seemed frozen on Rudy's face. "He comes an hour early. Remember?"

"Yes."

"Maybe he didn't get my letter."

"He always gets your letters."

"Yes. I know." He took the cigarette out of his mouth, examined it for a second, and dropped it onto the wooden platform. His hands hung at his sides. "Look, I am sorry."

"What are you sorry for now?" I said, pretending once more that I didn't know.

He looked down at the baggage. "Maybe we should not have come."

"What should we do now?"

Rudy's head snapped up. "They are here," he cried out.

I heard them shouting "Rudichka" before I saw the small group of his cousins and friends moving toward us.

Rudy laughed and waved both hands. "You see? You Americans. You give up so easy."

We piled into taxis. Rudy, baggage, and cousins in one, me in another, with the rest and some friends I remembered from Rudy's birthday party. Beno was sick and waiting for us at a cousin's home.

"A caravan!" Rudy shouted to me through his window.

We bumped over the cobblestoned streets to a new section of Chernovtsy, Demetrowia Street. Beno now lived with nieces and nephews who had taken him after Regina died.

The unlit foyer was black when we entered from the sunlit street. I smelled cabbage, kerosene and sweat. We left our luggage in the foyer of the apartment building. According to government regulations, we were supposed to continue shortly to the Hotel Cheremosh.

Cousin Alex felt for my hand to guide me. As my eyes adjusted he led me around chunks of concrete and stones that seemed to have fallen from the walls and ceilings. He squeezed my hand as though reading my mind.

"Dear God," I said under my breath.

Rudy's laugh came from the dark in front of me. "What, Schveetheart? Are you calling me?"

"No, it's nothing."

Alex held my hand tighter as we walked up flights of concrete steps, many of them cracked or missing. He called out something to Rudy and they all laughed.

"What did he say?" I asked.

"He apologized that the elevator is not running."

"Is there really an elevator?"

"Yes, there is. No electric though."

By the time we reached the top I had lost count of the floors. We walked into a small, neat apartment where bright sunlight streamed in from floor-to-ceiling windows. I realized with gratitude that although it was cold the apartment smelled fresh and clean. We took off our shoes and stood in the living room in our coats while Cousin Valentina poured vodka into tiny glasses.

"Is this your version of a cocktail party?" I asked Rudy.

"Cute. No, we are warming ourselves before we go in to see Beno. Do you have to go out?"

"Yes. I thought you'd never ask."

"Did you go at all on the train? Couldn't take it, huh?" The others looked over and asked what Rudy was laughing about.

"Don't you dare tell them." I said.

"Okay. Can I at least ask Valentina where the toilet is?"

Valentina took my hand and led me to a closet. I held my breath but exhaled when she lit a candle and I saw the bathroom was clean. I was thankful for the blue bowl of something that smelled like flowers. I wanted to grab Valentina and kiss her but I could only say spaciba, thank you. When I finished, I pulled the chain but nothing happened. A white enamel cup on a hook and a pail in the corner reminded me there was no water. The pail had a cover on it. I closed my eyes. I knew that if I lifted the lid and found dirty water I would faint. I lifted it slowly and scooped out the clean water.

"Hey kid, take it easy in there," Rudy whispered from the other side of the door. "It is my turn."

I changed places with Rudy. Valentina took me to another room to wash my hands. Again she lit a candle. She handed me a tiny piece of pink soap. I looked into her eyes and knew she had saved this bit of soap for me. She waited to pour water over my hands, cold water, then held out an embroidered towel. I searched her eyes again. They were filled with tears. I wanted to tell her she had dignity.

The men threw back another shot of vodka before Rudy gave the signal he was ready to go in to Beno. I walked next to Rudy. His face was pale. His hand was back on his chest.

In the darkened bedroom, other people stood silently against the walls. In the yellow light from a small lamp next to his bed, Beno looked dead. My first thought was that we were too late. But Rudy called out softly and the old man's eyes opened. He tried to lift his head from the pillow.

"Rudichka." Beno's voice seemed to shock everyone. "Rudichka," he sighed and fell back.

"Beno." Rudy moved quickly to the bed.

I stepped back against the door. I hugged myself to stop the shaking. I saw Rudy drop to his knees and bury his head in the covers before I put my hand over my eyes. Rudy's muffled sobs filled the room.

I understood when Beno whispered in Yiddish, "Rudichka, Rudichka, you have come to me."

The door opened behind me. I filed out with the rest of them and left Rudy alone with Beno.

CHAPTER 23

I stood by the living room window with my fist against my mouth and watched an old woman sweep the path to a cottage. A tall man walked through the wooden gate and greeted her with a wave. She brushed off a stone bench and they sat down. A plaque next to the cottage door caught the sun.

We waited a long time for Rudy to come out. The others stood in groups of twos and threes talking softly, drinking. Valentina walked around with a platter of thinly sliced bread covered with bits of cheese and herring. She tried to give me a slice. I couldn't eat.

I pointed out the window to the cottage downstairs and motioned that I wanted to know what it was. Valentina smiled and nodded. She thought a moment before she threw out her hands in desperation. I made a praying motion for her to please try. She sat down, bent over a table and pretended to write. She walked back to the window and pointed to the cottage. A place where people write. I asked if it was a school, an international word.

Valentina shook her head vigorously "No shkola." She pointed to Alex standing next to us and said "No Alex." Then she pointed to herself and me and said "Da." Alex is a man, we are women. "Damas? Women?" She wrinkled her brow, not knowing if I made the connection. She touched her breast. "Da?"

I said "women," and touched my own. Valentina's eyes came alive when she realized I understood. She pointed to me, then to the cottage and then motioned. I can write there. Women write there. She walked across the room to a bookshelf where she took down a book without looking at the title. She motioned again to me. Women who write books.

I made a square and pointed to the cottage again. "Billette," I said, trying to indicate I was interested in the sign, the plaque. Valentina looked downstairs. She shook her head that she didn't understand. "Billette, billette," I repeated, slapping my hand on the wall next to the window and then pointing down again. Valentina grinned. She took the book back to the shelf and searched for another. She brought me a tattered red one. She leafed through the yellowed pages and ran her hand over the scarred cover. She pointed to the author's name written in Cyrillic letters. She pointed down to the cottage. "Olga Kobylianska," she said.

I tried to repeat the name. Valentina laughed and repeated the name over until I got it right. Olga Kobylianska, a woman writer who lives in that house. I pointed to myself and motioned I wanted to talk to Olga Kobylianska. Valentina shook her head again. "No, no Olga Kobylianska." Valentina rested her head on her hands. Olga Kobylianska was dead.

"Oh."

Valentina got a stub of a pencil and a scrap of paper. She

wrote down 1863, then a line, then 1942. I wrote 1942, then a line and then a blank, pointing to myself.

She smiled and asked me something about months. "Mesas? Months?"

"Da," she nodded and pointed to me and 1942.

"January, February, March." I pointed to myself and repeated March. Valentina hesitated and stared at me. She looked confused as she wrote down a three for March, then a blank and then 1942. She handed me the pencil.

I reached into my bag on the table. I held out the royal blue booklet with the crest of the United States on the front. Valentina wiped her hands on her skirt, even though they were clean and carefully took the passport. She opened it to my picture. I pointed to my date of birth, March 22, 1942. Valentina took the pencil. She filled in the blank between the third month and 1942. Olga Kobylianska had died on March 21, 1942.

I tried to steady myself by studying the design etched into the brown leather of my shoes. I noticed how my feet were solidly placed on the floor, how the strip of color along the edge of my skirt made it clear and easy to see. I closed my eyes. The hushed voices around me pressed against my ears. A gust of wind rattled the window. I opened my eyes. Down in the street the old woman and the man were gone.

I stood by the window and waited for Rudy. Dim voices hummed in my ears and blurred faces filled the room. Yet I was alone. I folded my hands in my lap and looked up to the mirror over the sofa.

The message I got was as clear as it was the last time, when I had wandered away from the market on our first trip. I was exactly where I was supposed to be. Again I heard Rudy's voice that first day when he said he knew me. I heard his promise that he would take me home. And I remembered my promise to believe. I knew, in just that instant that I'd been waiting a long time for this moment, perhaps for my whole life. In my reflection my hair was silver from light that illuminated my head. There were dark shadows under my eyes from the long journey.

The door opened. Rudy walked out and shut the door silently. Alex reached his arm around Rudy's shoulders and led him to a couch where he sat back with his hand over his heart.

I knew Beno was dead.

I watched Rudy lift a glass and swallow its clear contents in one gulp. Someone held out another one. Then another. The color returned to Rudy's face. He took his hand off his chest and wiped his eyes.

I reached out to Valentina as she passed. "Taxi?" I asked.

"Rudy?" she responded.

"No Rudy." I motioned that I wanted the taxi to go to the hotel alone, and that I would come back. No one noticed our departure. She led me down the dark staircase where I took my one small suitcase and then we were out on the street. We walked up a steep hill to a very busy boulevard. Valentina smiled as she pointed up to the street sign on the corner of a building. The letters were not Cyrillic. I read "Uletsa Kobylianska." The street was named after that woman writer. I wondered if my heart was pounding because of our climb up the hill or because of the sign.

Valentina stopped a taxi. She told the driver to take me to the Hotel Cheremosh, paid him and showed me on her watch what time to come back. The driver shifted the gears and the taxi sprang down the boulevard. We passed those aging Austrian apartment buildings and I remembered that day Rudy, Beno and I walked down this street arm in arm to Regina's grave.

We stopped at a stop sign. An old woman raised her hand to wave. I raised my hand to wave back and realized I was still clutching Valentina's red book. A peasant's babushka tied tight around the old woman's creased face made her cheeks prominent and shiny. A straw basket filled high with potatoes weighed down her arm.

I sank back into the seat and sighed. Home.

The taxi driver opened the smudged glass door to the cement block Hotel Cheremosh. The three women standing at attention behind a counter looked as if they'd been waiting just for me. There were no other people in the cold lobby. I thought of judgment day and giggled. The driver looked back at me and frowned.

A woman stepped forward. "My name is Zoya," she said in English.

I reached out to shake her hand. "Oh, how wonderful, you speak English!"

Zoya flashed the warm smile that was distinctly Russian, gold teeth and all. "The driver wants to know when to come back for you."

"Oh, what time is it now? My watch says it's five-thirty, but that's in New York. Can he pick me up in about three hours?"

"Yes, of course. And can I change your watch for you? It is now twelve-thirty."

Zoya was silent on the way up the stairs. She glanced nervously at me from the corner of her eye. We reached a long shadowy corridor where the wall lamps were off. She opened the door to my room with a skeleton key and handed one to me.

"I am your perevodchik, your interpreter. I will stay with you wherever you go and help you with the language and any other needs you have. That is my job."

We stood in the doorway and looked at each other for a few seconds. I felt Zoya was prepared to either turn and leave quickly or engage in conversation.

She wore a gray suit over her slightly overweight body. The skirt was too tight around her hips and stomach. A soft pink blouse with its bow tied to the side was an attempt to look western. Long bleached blond hair accentuated her round, pretty face. Zoya was about forty years old, but the heavy makeup and thick red lipstick made her look older.

Her eagerness was a physical thing that reached out to me. Suddenly I felt secure, important.

I closed my eyes and breathed in the heaviness of Zoya's perfume. It was too much. Beno dying, Rudy's chest pain, that Olga cottage, the peasant woman in the red babushka waiting for the light to change. "A moment in time."

"What was that?" Zoya asked softly.

"Oh, I'm sorry. I didn't realize I was thinking out loud. I'm just so tired. What I said was, 'A moment in time.' Do you know what that means?"

"Yes, of course. And this is indeed a moment in time." Zoya hesitated. "For both of us."

"Zoya, I need to talk to you."

"Yes, I know."

"But I'm so tired."

"I will come back later." Zoya touched my arm. "Rest."

"Are you sure you'll still be here. Don't you go home? What if someone takes your place?"

"No, no. That is not the case. I will be here." Zoya walked away noiselessly on the long oriental runner.

"Zoya?"

She stopped but did not turn around.

"Zoya, do you know who Olga Kobylianska is?"

Zoya threw her head back and laughed. "Of course. Every

schoolchild knows Olga." She continued walking. Before she made the turn to the stairs she looked back at me.

Don't wave goodbye, I said silently. Please don't wave goodbye. She stood there for a second before she disappeared around the corner.

The room had shiny laminated furniture, heavy brown drapes, and two narrow beds separated by a low wooden table and set with stiff white linen. The two prints over the beds were both of orange and black boomerangs. I turned on the radio but there was no sound.

A warm bath in the huge old-fashioned tub will be the answer to everything, I thought. I felt the thin, dishcloth-type towels while I ran the icy water, and prayed it would get hot. The wall tiles were chipped and yellowed but the bathroom was clean. The harsh toilet paper was better than newspaper. I reached over to feel the still cold water just as it gurgled and spit and stopped.

"Great, just great," I said out loud.

I threw myself down on a bed. It was too cold to take anything off. I was still wearing my coat. I rolled myself in the blanket and stared up at the cracks in the ceiling. My bones ached. I wanted to stay awake long enough to sort through what was happening. I moved the blanket up over my mouth like Rudy taught me and felt the miracle of my warm breath. Rudy loved to say his breath was his heat in the camps in the winter.

"Funny," I'd say to him. "Real funny."

"Actually," he said, "it wasn't funny. Some people didn't have warm breath. Some people were dead."

I woke with a start to the harsh ringing of the red plastic phone next to my head. It was Zoya reminding me it was time to get up.

I fell back on my pillow. I couldn't focus on any of the

dreams but I know I'd seen my father, the old men in City Island, Beno, Regina, my grandmother Bessie. Rudy's mother, the cousin with her blue baby in the snow, they were there too.

I started to fall back to sleep. I was just reaching that point somewhere between sleep and being awake when I saw the figure of a woman at the foot of my bed. In a second she faded away.

A new energy pulsated through my arms and legs. I threw off the blanket, jumped up from the bed and splashed cold water on my face.

I changed into the long flowered skirt and embroidered linen blouse that Rudy loved even though they were too thin for winter. I pulled up black wool leggings under my skirt.

So much for spring, I thought as a light snow fell outside my window. I stood in the doorway thinking I forgot something. My long red coat with its matching scarf was thrown over my shoulders. My gloves were in my pocket. My purse, tissues for toilet paper, medication if my stomach didn't hold out, an extra pair of socks. I had my reading glasses, my passport. Money! I had no money. I realized it didn't matter, no one would take my dollars now anyhow. The old days were gone, and the black market with it. "This is it," I whispered to the empty room.

CHAPTER 24

Zoya stepped back and spread her hands as I approached in the lobby. "What happened to you?" she asked. "Look at you, so refreshed."

"Oh, it's a long story."

"That's good. I have all the time in the world. And I love long stories."

"That's good. Because you see, Zoya, this is it." I expected Zoya to respond by asking me what I meant. She didn't. She merely nodded and pointed the way to the restaurant. "After you," she said.

Zoya was a great listener. She seemed to eat every word. A knowing smile never left her round face. There seemed to be no surprises for her in my story.

The taxi driver appeared, but we told him to come back. When we finally stood to leave the hotel many hours later, I had dragged Zoya from my childhood in the Bronx, to my grandmother Bessie, born in the neighboring village of

Sadagura. I told her about the baby girl Bessie had left there, conceived in a love affair with a gypsy man. Zoya's expression didn't change when I relived how Bessie had put me into a trance and pretended I was that girl she'd left behind. I told her about Rudy's childhood in Chernovtsy, the camps he'd been in, our life together in New York, the gambling, the drinking, the search for the best gypsy music. I described my move to City Island and my time there alone. Zoya's eyes filled with tears when I confessed my great love for Rudy. I was breathless as my story closed around Beno and Regina, and how I had just learned about Olga Kobylianska.

I stopped myself before I told her about the ring.

I rested my head in my hands. Zoya waited silently. "Do you think I'm another crazy American?" I asked.

"No, not at all."

"Well, maybe if I tell you the best part."

"Yes, okay, the best part." Zoya's eyes were alive with excitement. "Tell me the best part."

"Do you know when Olga Kobylianska died?"

"No, not exactly. I know it was around 1941. No, it was 1942. I know too it was in March. Every year we have a national broadcast to commemorate her, to remember the day."

"It was March 21, 1942."

"That is very nice of you to know our national heroine so well."

"But do you know when I was born?"

Zoya stared at me.

"March 22, 1942."

"You mean when Olga Kobylianska died?"

"No, when I was born. I was born the day after Olga died.

Zoya folded her plump hands on the linen table cloth.

"Zoya, say something."

"I am thinking you Americans think things like this are so strange. They are not strange to our people. Not at all."

"There is something I must do."

"Yes, I would think so."

"But what? I need you, Zoya. Please tell me you will help me."

"It would be an honor."

"Good, then come." I said. "It's time I introduce you to Rudy."

Alex let us in. Someone on the couch was covered with a mound of blankets. Valentina bent over the person with a steaming cup. For a second I thought it was Beno, but it was Rudy.

"Rudy." I threw down my purse and ran to him without taking off my shoes. His ashen face was vacant. His eyes were closed. "Rudy, it's me."

"Schveetheart, you've come back to me."

"Where else would I go on a night like this?"

Rudy reached out for my hand and kissed it with the same warm lips. "Where have you been? I've been waiting so long."

"Oh, come on now. I had to go check into the hotel, or you know they would come looking for us."

"How's the new hotel, Cheremosh?"

"The same as the others."

"Cold?"

"What else?" I laughed.

Rudy laughed too. The color came back to his face. Valentina offered the cup again and Rudy lifted himself on his elbow. "Ah, you can't beat their chai.

"Too bad you don't drink their tea more often."

"I will. From now on, I promise."

"Right. I know. Look, look who's here."

Rudy looked past me at Zoya. There was a deep silence as he checked her out. He looked back at me with that sparkle in his eye.

"Son of a bitch," I said in a low voice so Zoya would not hear me.

"What did you say that for?" Rudy's faint smile said he knew the answer.

"You know why. You know everything, remember?"

Rudy moved his head closer to me. "She's a little chubby, don't you think?"

"You must be kidding. What does that have to do with anything? She's our translator."

"I don't need a translator, remember?"

"Well then, what do you need?"

Rudy glanced at Zoya again and fell back on his cushion.

"I asked what do you need?"

"Beno's gone you know."

"Yes, I know."

"Beno's gone, Regina's gone. My mother is gone. They are all gone and you ask what do I need?"

"I'm still here you know. At least I'm here." I didn't want to sound like I was begging, but I did.

"Look kid, just leave me alone for now. You can't give me what I need. Nobody can."

I backed away from the couch. I turned so Rudy wouldn't see the tears. I was ashamed of my anger, but I couldn't help it.

I walked to the window and looked down at Olga's house. Zoya and Valentina came up behind me. "Look, Zoya, you see?" The women exchanged words and I heard the dates again. "So." Zoya's whisper was filled with excitement. "We will go, no?"

I looked back at Rudy who was snoring gently with the

cover over his mouth. "But isn't it too late? There won't be anybody there now."

"No, no. I sent a message while you were asleep. He is there, waiting for you."

"Who's waiting?"

"Vladimir is waiting."

"Who is that?"

"Vladimir, the curator of the museum. He dedicates his life to Olga Kobylianska."

The amber lights of the shops' kerosene lanterns spread peacefully over the covering of new snow. But the stately old lampposts I remembered from previous trips were not lit.

Four teenage boys sang a lively tune in deep bass voices as they marched briskly, arm in arm, down the road in front of us. Zoya beamed. "You see how happy they are? No heat, no lights, no water. Still they sing."

"You have so little."

"Do not sound so pained. We will have our country now."

"Didn't you always, in a way?"

"No. First there were the Hungarians, then the Austrians, then Romanians, then Russians."

"I must apologize. I know nothing of your politics. You know how we Americans are. Forgive me."

"If you are interested in Olga Kobylianska, then you must know more." Zoya stretched out her arm. "Look around you. You see, her dream has come true. Ukraine will be an independent country. This is what she lived for. In a way, it is what she died for."

Zoya stopped walking while I peered into a barely illuminated shop. A young couple paused near us to look in the window where there was a small pyramid of cans. A round, dark bread, exposed to the snow, stuck out from a basket the man carried. The woman pulled a child on a sled. The teenage boys stopped. I heard dosvidaniya, goodbye. The boy leaving kissed each of the others on both cheeks.

"Do you see that in America?" Zoya asked.

"Teenagers, boys, walking arm in arm, kissing each other goodbye? I don't think so."

Zoya smiled. "And these boys are not what you say, gay. These boys have love for each other. It is the love of brothers, all of them."

I looked around me at the dismal street.

"I know what you look for. Color, of course. But we are a new country. In the meantime look at that child's cheeks. There is your color. And that bread, that lovely dark bread. Black like our soil." Zoya nodded her head.

"Ukraine has the blackest, richest soil in the world."

"Really? I wonder how many people know that."

"*Zemlya, The Land*, that was one of Olga Kobylianska's best stories. She believed in the land, and the peasant, especially in the peasant."

I remembered the peasant in the babushka waiting at the corner.

"But let us go. It is cold for you to stand here." Zoya slipped her arm through mine and we proceeded to the cottage I'd seen from Valentina's window.

The path that had been cleared earlier by the woman with the broom was covered again with snow. Zoya knocked hard on the front door. Tiny crystal icicles hung from the edge of the brass plaque. I moved my head closer to listen for voices and my cheek brushed the wooden door. In an instant, that market day with Regina and Rudy came back to me again. I saw myself wandering away, down that quiet, mysterious street, this street, sitting on that bench where the old woman and man sat earlier.

"Oh, there's no one here." I whispered.

"Of course they are here. Do not worry. Come, we will go to the back."

I followed Zoya through the narrow path. We passed a many-paned window where a spotlight lit the back of a statue. Olga Kobylianska's hair was knotted in a tight bun. There was pride in her erect spine, in the way her head was tilted up.

Zoya turned and came back to me. "That, my dear, is your Olga Kobylianska."

A gust of wind howled around the side of the cottage and caught me unexpectedly. My eyes filled with tears. Zoya reached out to grab me.

"I'm sorry, it's just that so much has . . ."

"Why do you apologize so?" Zoya's voice was soft with sympathy. "It's all right, go ahead."

I wiped my cheeks with my gloved hands as I laughed and cried at the same time. Snowflakes stuck to my eyelashes. My nose was running. "What a mess I am. How can I go in like this?"

Zoya handed me a white embroidered handkerchief.

"You know, nobody uses these in America anymore." I dabbed at my tears.

"They don't have to." Zoya laughed. "In your country you have paper."

She knocked on the back door although it was open. It was as cold in the hallway as it was outside. The old woman with the broom was now sitting behind a desk that held a roll of green tickets and a dish with coins. She looked up with a sour face and adjusted a rough wool scarf over her head and shoulders. We seemed to have disturbed her sleep. She mumbled and tore off two tickets. Zoya said something. The old woman shook her head and shrugged.

"What is it?" My shocked voice surprised me. "What's wrong?"

"Nothing at all. Vladimir went to dinner. He will be back shortly. Come, we will sit by the oven and wait."

"But shouldn't we buy tickets anyhow? How much are they?"

"It is nothing. The equivalent of your nickel perhaps."

"I will give a contribution, something larger, much larger." As I reached into my purse I remembered I didn't have money.

"Don't worry about it. Later will be fine."

The walls in Vladimir's tiny office were lined with books. Two desks overflowed with papers. On one shelf a solitary, lit candle illuminated a miniature, framed photograph of Olga Kobylianska, and next to it, a small black book.

"This room is warmer than anywhere else I've been today," I said.

"It is not always so. Vladimir knew you were coming. He must have prepared the room for you."

"That's so embarrassing, Zoya. It's only me."

"Exactly." Zoya opened her coat buttons. "It is you."

I sat down and studied Olga's determined mouth. Shadows from the flickering candle played over her face making the intelligent eyes move. "Zoya, what is this book about?"

Zoya opened the book. "It is Olga's diary, written in her own handwriting. Shall I read it to you while we wait?"

"Oh, Zoya, please, it would mean everything to me."

Zoya moved closer to the light. "I will do my best."

CHAPTER 25

February 12, 1939

I am just returned from the Cernatu train station. I am grateful that tonight I have the strength to fill a page or two. Someone must write about what is taking place here. Now that the Germans are in Chernovtsy the politics are indeed over. It is only a matter of time and all will be lost, gone.

There were so many deportees in the station tonight that there was no place for them to sit. Jews, gypsies, took turns sitting on the floor. I did the best I could, moving among the people in spite of the pain that has become one with my breath. It arches up my back, spreads through my arms, down my legs. But I tried not to slide my foot along the floor. I do not want them to pity me. Let them think I am just old.

It does not matter. Where they go, nothing matters. The cattle cars waiting in the yard were as silhouetted coffins against the waning light. It is hopeless, too late to help them. I can only come here and pretend there is hope.

I heard my name travel through the stale air in whispers. Olga has come to see us; Olga says we are to have courage, to hope for a better time.

This is how I know I am succeeding and that I must keep going, every day if possible until the Germans manage to stop me.

It is amazing how these deportees hang onto their dignity. A man in a wrinkled suit had all the buttons done. The brooch on the velvet dress was still straight in its place. And the silent children, saplings bent in surrender against their elders. Their faces were already with sad eyes. Their mouths formed tight patient lines.

I saw a boy standing in the corner. His face was a frozen mask but I could see he knew everything. I wondered for a second if my son would have looked like him. But then I dare not wonder. Wondering uses up time, the only commodity we have now.

The lice make misery so much worse for these people. The boy reached to scratch his head with one hand while the other worked furiously at his ankle. His slight body, perhaps he was ten years old, supported such a regal head. His eyes look beyond the wall, out to another place. He went back to his mother and she clutched him to her side. I was able to bend and touch his head. The last of daylight filtered through the high, streaked window above us. A shaft of light fell on his smooth young brow, on my wrinkled hand. What difference does it make, I think, in that place where ten becomes seventy, and seventy becomes a hundred.

The boy looked at me. The tight thin lips made his mouth almost disappear. "Little prince," I whispered in Ukrainian. No response. I repeated it in Romanian. No response. Russian. I wondered how to say it in Yiddish. But then he mumbled. A word, not a word, a swallowed breath escaped the tight lips. I saw the others around him look away.

I have heard of the secret word of the Jews. As I struggled with it, the boy's eyes came alive with a spark. The corner of his fine mouth lifted slightly. And then suddenly he murmured, Amchoor. Yes, Amchoor, I repeated. From nowhere a tear appeared on his pale cheek. I brushed it away, studying again the contrast of my hand against his cheek. Time was running out. Perhaps I could save just this one. I grabbed his arm and helped him up with a strength I did not know I had. The mother's arm fell away. His old, serious eyes looked into my soul. I lifted his cold hand to the light. The childish nails were cracked and broken, the creases and cuts embedded with dirt. I held it against my chest. The mother rested on a bony arm in the space he had left. I wondered if he knew she was dying. I asked an old man to take the boy out to the latrine and bent to the mother. She did not move, but her eyes turned to see me. So she knew I was there. I eased myself down beside her so she could talk in my ear. She moved her head closer. Her words were low, strained.

I am Eva, who are you, she asked. I am Olga. I was afraid she would ask me to do something for her. Nothing can be done here anymore. Where is my boy? she asked. He had to go out, I told her. He will be right back. And then she said, I need to trust you. I have heard your name. There is no one else. My son is only twelve. He will die without me. I know it. I heard him say it. He planned our escape. They found us. We are back.

Eva was making weak, sobbing sounds that came from deep inside her. I pulled her close and patted her back. Only a thin coat covered her slight shoulders, her shivering body. The smell of evil closed in around us. Her hand moved along the damp floor to a pile of rags. She pushed her hand into a tied bundle. In the dim light I saw her fist close around a packet wrapped with a sliver of colorless ribbon. You must hold something for me, for my boy, she said. Our survival depends on it. I have kept it for these last days but you see how it is. After this is over you will give it to him. He is the last one. Show him the secret, the power inside, as I show it to you.

The ring Eva held up before my face was encrusted with rubies. Her thumb moved along the band. When she pressed the side of the jeweled top it sprung open. She clicked it closed.

I pushed the ring into my shoe. You must take care of my boy, she said. You must not let him die. Be his mother.

Promise me you will not let him die.

I will not let him die, I promised. I am about to die myself. What does a broken promise matter?

CHAPTER 26

Zoya's voice and the warmth of the room had put me in a daze where I could see the boy and Olga reaching out to pat his head. But then Zoya's shout cut through my dream. "He is here!" I opened my eyes to see her jump out of her chair.

Vladimir smoothed his hair and turned for Zoya to introduce me. He took both my hands in his, looked into my eyes and kissed me on both cheeks. When he stepped back his cologne and the smell of alcohol filled the space between us. He said something to Zoya. They both smiled at me.

Straight dark hair swept across Vladimir's forehead. A thin belt held stylish, pleated trousers around his slender waist. The soft brown moccasins looked American-made. Vladimir felt his mustache continuously. He looked about forty years old so I knew immediately he was not around when Olga was alive.

"Come, Vladimir will show you Olga's home." Zoya stepped aside to let us pass. "This is just an addition to the cottage you know."

Vladimir offered me his arm, squeezed mine tight against him and patted my hand as we walked.

He threw open a door at the other end of the hallway. We were in Olga Kobylianska's study.

The elegant room was sparsely furnished. Colorful oriental rugs partially covered shiny wood floors. The piano in the corner was open. We walked across the study to a glass cabinet constructed to protect the neatly arranged articles on Olga's writing table. I was disappointed by the ordinary pens, an early black telephone, a silver letter opener and an open journal. A bracelet and watch rested on a strip of blue velvet, looking as though they were just put there by their owner for the night. There was a corked bottle of water.

"What is that in the bottle?"

Zoya translated my question. Vladimir answered, "It was Olga's dream to go to the Black Sea but she could not afford it. Her friend Lesya, also a famous writer and poet, sent this water from the Black Sea. By the time Olga earned enough money from her writing to buy this house she was too old to travel. And so she kept that bottle right there when she wrote."

I seemed to be somewhere between the world I'd just heard of from the diary and what was around me. A familiarity in this room dissipated my confusion as quickly as it had started. Everything was exactly what it should be, and where it should be.

In the next room a blue and red carpet hung on the wall behind Olga's narrow bed. Vladimir saw me look up at a picture of Olga over the bed. He told Zoya to inform me that this was not Olga but her mother. I asked about the trundle bed partially pulled out from under Olga's bed. He said her nephews came to visit often. They loved her bedtime stories and slept right there next to her.

"Nephews? What about her own children?"

"No, no children. She never married."

"Really?"

"It is a rather sad story. You didn't get to it in the diary. You see there was a man. Actually there were many men, but this one was Olga's great love. He was a writer too, a poet. They were so much in love. Everyone in Chernovtsy knew it. When the time came for them to marry Vitalie said he expected Olga to give up her writing. He wanted her to take care of their home, their children and especially him. He wanted her assurance that he could go on writing undisturbed."

"In other words," I said, "he expected Olga to be a housewife?"

"Exactly. She said no. Olga would never consent to such an agreement. And that was the end of that."

"How sad."

"She made the best of it. She was involved in the politics of the time, writing controversial, nationalistic pieces advocating for a unified, independent Ukraine. Unfortunately she got herself into a lot of trouble with the Nazis. They were going to court-martial her to keep her quiet. Imagine, an old woman like that. By then she could hardly walk.

"She also believed in what she called the aristocracy of the spirit. She was so much before her time. She knew women had rights. When the peasants beat their wives and threw them out into the street, Olga took them in and nursed them back to health."

"Her writing was superb." Vladimir's hands were pressed together as in prayer. "Her subjects were the rich soil, the land, the trees, and most of all the peasants and gypsies that lived in her town when she was a child. *On Sunday She Gathered Herbs* is about an outspoken, independent woman."

Vladimir and Zoya stared at me in silence waiting for my next question.

"How is it that nobody knows of this woman?"

"Aha," exclaimed Zoya. "Now you have it. That is the problem. Her work is read all over our region. We produce her plays. Our children study her work in the schools. Later I will take you to the music theater named after her. The United Nations even issued a special stamp in her honor in 1963. It would have been her one hundredth birthday. The pity is she has never been translated into English."

"I was trying to get the dates straight in my head. When Olga died in 1942 the war was still on?"

Now Vladimir talked even faster. "Yes, yes of course and oh how she suffered for the people. She knew what was going on. Do you know that as old and infirm as she was, she hired a car to carry her to the other side of town to the Chernatu station? It was there they held the Jews and gypsies before moving them to the camps in Transnystria. She did this for months, going back and forth."

"Why? What could she do for them?"

"It is said she brought baskets of food, but it was not really the food. Everyone knew Olga Kobylianska, and loved her. That is how she got to see the deportees to begin with. Even the guards held her in such high regard that, I mean, you can just see her." Vladimir's eyes were on fire. "A crippled old woman, bent over her cane, gets out of her car. She walks through the snow with two people trailing behind with baskets. One day Olga arrived at the opening to the gate they set up around the station. A new guard was on duty. He was young and filled with eagerness over his important position. He raised his hand to stop her. Olga paused momentarily, straightened herself, held her head up high and kept walking. It is said that the, how do you call it, the atmosphere around her was such that no one dared approach her.

"She brought more than food. She brought hope.

"She was independence, strength, endurance to everyone who knew her. You see, if Olga said it would be all right, they believed it would be all right. If she said survive, they would survive. It was that simple, that important. She knew it."

I was light-headed. Zoya and Vladimir must have sensed it. They turned and left, shutting the door behind them.

I rested my head on the back of an overstuffed settee in the corner of her bedroom. I picked up Olga's cane that rested against the wall and ran my fingers along the smooth wood.

My mind was full of their words, survival, independence, hope. I closed my eyes and saw the train station, the same one Rudy and I always arrived in. I saw Olga walking through the snow, her head high.

I admired the iron gas lamps that had been converted to electric but were now useless. A crying wind drove dense snow against the window, making faint wet sounds. I remembered Rudy's words. "There is survival and there is survival." And I suddenly realized that even from that first day, when he promised to take me home, every struggle, slip and turn of our lives together had been divinely planned toward this moment.

CHAPTER 27

Rudy was still asleep when we returned to the apartment. His shallow breathing filled the room. I asked if he had been awake at all. Valentina shook her head.

"Rudy, it's me. I'm back. Wake up."

Rudy opened his eyes.

"Come now, sit up. I need to talk to you. So much has happened."

Rudy didn't move.

"Please, don't scare me like this. Say something."

"I'm okay."

"Show me." He lifted himself to his elbow and moaned.

"My God, what's the matter?"

"It's the pain in my chest."

"Oh, no. I thought you said you're okay."

"You don't sound very sympathetic."

"Look how much you've had to drink. Did you think one

cup of chai would be enough to cure you? How many times have we been through this?"

"This is different."

"How many times have you said that too?" Despite how scared I was, I tried not to sound angry.

"Look, I know you're angry." Rudy's voice softened. "I'm sorry, okay? It's Beno. I used to be able to deal with the pain. It was my middle name. I can't take any more."

"Quite a speech, Rudy. I'm impressed with your honesty."

"Don't you dare call me honest." He crooked his finger for me to bend over. "It's just that, I mean, can't you have pity on a dying man?"

"Oh is that it? You're hung over and you expect me to believe you're dying?"

"Believe me."

"I don't."

"Then would you consider marrying me?"

"What did you say?"

"Marry me. Now do you believe me?"

I stood up and looked down at Rudy. His good blue shirt, wrinkled from traveling, had wine stains on the front. His eyes were bloodshot. "Let's go back to the hotel and talk about this. You need a shave and a shower."

Zoya's cough behind me reminded me there was no shower, no shave with warm water, nothing but a cold room.

"I want to stay here." Rudy's voice was stronger. "I belong here tonight."

"We must go back to the hotel. You know how they are."

"It's all right, you go. Tomorrow we'll talk. I'll be in better shape tomorrow. You will see."

I let my body relax as I realized I needed to be alone.

Zoya and I didn't talk in the taxi. I rested my head against the seat and kept my eyes closed all the way back to the hotel. In the lobby I asked if I could get hot water, even if only a pitcher.

Zoya formed a huddle with the others. She turned with a smile. "Some government big shots are staying at the hotel tonight so they have used the generator for a sauna in the basement. You can use it if you wish."

I rushed up to my room, grabbed what I needed and raced down to the basement. Zoya waited at the end of a dark corridor. She pushed a pass and robe into my hands, kissed me on both cheeks and said good night.

An attendant in a white coat sat at a desk reading a magazine. He looked up for a second, obviously to see if I was the American he was waiting for. I held up the pass and he went back to his reading. I stripped in the frigid dressing room, wrapped myself in the robe and wandered through a maze of corridors to the sauna room. The delight of wet, warm steam was beyond any expectation. The hot shower next door and the rough piece of soap, although it made no lather, delighted me. I would bring Rudy here tomorrow no matter what happens. This would certainly bring him back to life.

Back in my room I dove under the bed covers. Huge snowflakes flew against my rattling windows. My body tingled from the sauna, and the shower. I was determined not to worry about Rudy. As I drifted off to sleep my last thought was that somehow everything from now on was going to be about me.

I overslept but felt wonderful. I dressed in my warmest clothes and went down to find Zoya.

"Coffee is ready," she said. I didn't tell her that what they called coffee in her country would never make it in America.

The government big shots, in dark suits, were having breakfast and arguing. Their presence explained why the dining room was warmer than it had been the day before.

I was about to refuse the runny eggs, cold hard roll and slice of dry salami that I knew was coming, until Zoya asked if she could eat my breakfast. It took a long time to arrive. We chatted about life in America. Is it true that people sleep on the street? Is it true that people get hundreds of dollars every month from welfare and unemployment insurance? Is it true that we have cars costing thirty thousand dollars? Is it true that we call our president by his first name? Zoya was a big-eyed child with her nose pressed against a store window.

What I wanted to tell her was that I was more impressed with the rosy-cheeked child, the black bread, the graceful way Valentina served us. "You have dignity here," was all I could think of to say.

With her brow wrinkled in concentration over the food, and her pinky finger delicately extended, Zoya dipped a roll into the loose egg whites. "Dignity indeed," she said, "as I eat your breakfast."

I planned my day out loud while Zoya ate. First, I would walk back to Valentina's apartment instead of taking a taxi. If Rudy cooperated we would come back here so I could take him to the sauna. If he did not cooperate I wanted to go back to Olga's house.

I told Zoya I would be fine alone but she insisted on walking with me. We went to her office for her walking shoes and coat. There was a dusty manual typewriter on her desk along with two well-sharpened pencils and a neat pile of papers. A curling poster of the Carpathian Mountains was the only adornment. Zoya blushed and said it was not tourist season.

It was a business day in Chernovtsy. It was still snowing. People squeezed past each other. Their faces intent on getting where they were going reminded me of New York City, only here there were long lines everywhere.

"It is not easy, life here. It will take us time. Mother Russia,

Moscow has given us, how do you Americans say, the squeeze."
Zoya clutched her hand tight in the air to illustrate the
strangulation.

"How?"

"She let us go with no struggle, no war. Just cut us, loose as
you say. Now there is no fuel. It was as if they said, go, freeze
to death, starve to death too. You want an independent free
Ukraine?"

"Oh. Is that what it's all about? I had no idea."

Zoya's laughter had a bitter ring. "Nobody had any idea."

"This couldn't possibly be what Olga Kobylianska had in
mind either."

"No, she had independence in mind, but with the fuel and
the food I'm sure."

We stopped in a small park where small groups of mostly
young people talked and argued. Animated, gloved hands flew
about in the frigid air. Exhaled cigarette smoke created white
clouds above their heads.

"Politics?" I asked.

Zoya nodded.

"There was something up there last time Rudy and I were
here." I pointed to the long concrete block at the top of the
park. "Weren't there statues?"

"Lenin and Stalin. We took them down. Actually, we knocked
them down. Olga would have approved of that. But as to the
rest of it, I think she was interested in the country belonging to
the peasants. She saw the future of our country in their hands,
their work, the soil."

"What happened?"

We started walking again. "Look, see those farmers?" Zoya
pointed to an old couple selling potatoes and onions from the
back of their horse-drawn wagon. Two children bundled in

blankets and straw watched from the wagon bed. "There are your peasants, I mean Olga's peasants. They were young in Olga's day. Now the young people turn away from such a life. Soil means hard work."

CHAPTER 28

The street where Valentina lived was deserted. "I guess everyone is working," I said.

Zoya laughed. "Or standing in line someplace for food."

She walked into the hallway first. I was holding the door open for her when I heard someone coming down the stairs. I saw the shiny black patent leather shoes first, then the bottom of a full skirt. A baby whimpered.

I was face to face with a gypsy. Zoya mumbled something under her breath. The girl hesitated. She stared at me with wide frightened eyes for a second before bolting out the door.

"Who was that?" I turned to watch the girl run down the street. The colors in the swirl of her skirt contrasted sharply with the gray buildings. A baby bounced in the sling across her back.

Zoya waved her hand. "Don't pay any mind. She probably has half the money in this building hidden in her filthy skirt. They have special pockets for stealing, you know."

"But where did she come from?"

"From the other side of the river, the Sadagura side. That's where they live. What she was doing here, I don't know. She probably stole something somewhere and found a customer here. You never know with these people. They are always up to something. They steal something from you and then try to sell it back to you."

"The baby. She was a little girl herself, but she had a baby."

"They all do. That's the problem. Come, let us go up."

Rudy was holding court at the head of Valentina's dining room table. The brown flannel bathrobe he wore was so out of character I burst out laughing.

"Good morning, Schveetheart! He stood up and kissed me on both cheeks.

His freshly shaved face and the scent of cologne delighted me. "I like the new hair style."

Rudy ran his hand over his plastered hair and winked. "You should see the rest of me," he winked.

"Mmm, when?"

"Would you believe they filled an old-fashioned tin tub with hot water. It took them all night. They went up and down the stairs carrying pails of water from the faucet down in the courtyard. When the electric went on at midnight for two hours they heated up the water."

"Rudy, how could you?"

"How could I what? I gave them something to live for."

Zoya nodded her head. "He's probably right," she said under her breath with a smile.

Valentina served a grand breakfast of crusty black bread, herring, onions and green tomatoes she pickled herself. A breathless old woman knocked on the door just as we sat down. She lifted the end of the checkered cloth covering a basket to display butter and cheese. Valentina picked out what she wanted and stepped back. Rudy said something that made the peasant woman smile a toothless grin and proceed to unload almost everything in her basket onto the table. Rudy put his hand into the bathrobe pocket and paid her without looking at the money. She was at the door when he jumped up and whispered in her ear. She reached into a sack over her shoulder and brought up a small glass jar which Rudy then held up to the light. "Ahh," he sighed and everyone laughed.

"Another cure-all?" I asked.

"No, no," Rudy answered in an excited, high-pitched voice. "This one really works. I'll bet you don't know what this is." Carefully he unwound the string holding a piece of white cloth around the neck of the jar. "Come, come, Miss America. Try this." He held out a spoon.

They all watched as I opened my mouth and closed my eyes tight to put on a show. I expected it would be sweet like whipped cream or ice cream. I screwed up my face when I swallowed the unbelievably sour cream.

"See? She loves it," Rudy said in English. I heard Zoya translating to the others.

"So," he asked. "What is it? What do you think?"

"I don't know."

"Sour milk. Try to get that in your America."

"I don't know how I lived without it."

Rudy was in fine form again. I allowed myself one innocent moment to admire the color in his face before I looked down at the vodka bottle. At least he wasn't drunk.

He saw me eye the bottle. "Don't get excited. I needed to get my heart started up again. That's all. No big deal. I'm okay."

"Look, I have so much to talk to you about. So much has happened," I said. "And we're supposed to get married, remember?"

"Yes, yes, we will talk, I promise. But not now. I am still not myself. It's not the same without Beno. It still hurts. I have to put on this little show here, for them. You know how it is."

Rudy held a full glass high in the air. The chairs scraped on the wooden floor as the others stood and raised their glasses, too. Rudy stretched his free arm out straight in front of him. "Heil Hitler!" he shouted. I looked around the table for shocked faces. There were none.

Rudy looked ridiculous in the bathrobe, the worn house slippers and his plastered hair, but I couldn't help it. "I love you Rudy."

He turned in my direction, clicked his heels and raised his glass to me. "To you, Schveetheart!"

I checked at the window to see if the door to Olga's house was open yet. The color in Rudy's cheeks darkened as he belted back another glass of vodka. Everyone was laughing at his jokes. I watched as his hand gradually moved up his chest.

I couldn't remember one time I successfully stopped Rudy from drinking. And yet, once again I bent over his shoulder and whispered, "Rudy, please, that's enough."

"Enough what? See how they love me?" Rudy stretched his arm out and pushed me back. "Look, kid, go find someplace we can go tonight. Let's take them all out. There isn't that much time left. Ask your Zoya. She knows someplace with good music, gypsy music. Right Zoya? Make reservations. You're good at that."

I felt the tears well up. "Zoya, let's get out of here."

Valentina walked us to the door.

"Zoya, tell her I need air." Valentina smiled and nodded that she understood. She started to close the door when I remembered.

"Zoya, please ask her if that gypsy girl was coming from here."

Valentina shook her head.

"Ask her please, has she ever seen a gypsy girl in this building or outside."

Valentina said no again, but then she said something else.

Zoya looked embarrassed. "Valentina is reminding me that the gypsies do not come into town. They stay by the River Prut."

"But Zoya, you did see her too."

"I know. Maybe it was just one of those things."

"What things?"

"I don't know." Zoya sounded mildly annoyed.

"Okay then. Let's go."

CHAPTER 29

It was no longer snowing. Trees glistened in the weak noontime sun. Every step we took cracked the thin layer of ice covering the snow. In seconds my face stiffened from the frigid air. Zoya pulled me along to Olga's cottage where the old woman waved us in.

Vladimir was waiting for us in his snug office. His eyes danced with excitement as he brought some papers from behind his back, two pages of an English translation of Olga's work, *Impromptu Fantasy*. I could take it back to the hotel to read, but not back to America. I did not ask about copying machines. I didn't want to embarrass them.

There were loud voices and laughter in the hallway. Vlamimir said it was a group of German businessmen, and that Olga's cottage was a routine stop on the city tour. I asked if he was supposed to join the group, to show them around. He shook his head but I knew he was being polite so I said I needed to spend time alone.

I settled with Olga's story next to Vladimir's oven while he and Zoya went to meet the group. I was surrounded by a light warm blanket of peace.

Olga's writing style, her simple yet profound language was so introspective, so personal I felt she was opening her heart to me.

Just as I finished, a twig broke outside the window. My first thought was that a branch snapped from the cold. But then there was a vague metallic sound, like the clinking of bracelets, and then a baby cried. I jumped up and pressed my face against the cold glass. I saw only Olga's garden covered over in deep drifts of snow.

I went back to Olga's study and stood in the corner watching the Germans. The nasal voice of their tour guide and his coarse-sounding words filled the elegant room. One of the visitors absentmindedly rested his hand on the glass case over Olga's desk. Vladimir took one long step to reach him. He poked the German in the shoulder and motioned for him to remove his hand. Then Vladimir pulled a handkerchief from his pocket and proceeded to gingerly rub off the fingerprints.

As soon as the tour was over I reminded Zoya about Rudy's request for a restaurant. "He wants gypsy music tonight."

"That can be arranged," she said. Valentina told you the gypsies are not allowed in town but this is not entirely true. A new restaurant, called the Retro, just opened. I hear there is a young gypsy violinist who plays like no other. For this they are allowed to come into Chernovtsy from Sadagura. To play music they are always accepted."

"Did I tell you I know about Sadagura? Did I tell you my grandmother was born there?"

Zoya nodded.

"My grandmother, born in the next town, walking distance from where Rudy was born. You know when I first asked Rudy where Sadagura was, he laughed and said it was where he and the other boys used to go to play soccer before the war."

"So many coincidences, as you Americans say."

"You say it like you don't believe in coincidences."

"I don't. Everything happens for a reason."

"You must be right because I feel so close to, to something." I was about to tell Zoya about the sounds outside his office window, when we were interrupted by Vladimir who had so much more to say about Olga's life. We left the cottage when it became obvious Zoya was exhausted from the translating.

When we got back to Valentina's, Zoya explained to Rudy that it was time to get himself and the luggage back to the hotel. Rudy was drunk but seemed to sober up somewhat when she said the authorities there were asking for him.

I got him into a bedroom to get his clothes together.

"They love me." Rudy looked at himself in the mirror. "You see how they love me? I am just what they need."

"Yes, I know. But I need you too. Remember? You said you would not forget me."

"Ah, my Schveetheart." He pulled me down on the bed. "I did not forget you. I will never forget you." He slid his hand under my sweater and felt the many layers I was wearing. "What is this? Where are you?"

"Look, you brought me here. You brought me to this freezing country where I have to wear three sweaters because there's no heat. And long underwear, and two pairs of socks."

Rudy's hand fell back on the bed. "I am not that drunk, you know. I brought you home. You wanted to be here. You needed to be here, remember?"

"I don't seem to recall," I lied. Once again I'd underestimated him. Even when he had too much to drink, he knew everything. "We must get back to the hotel. You heard what Zoya said."

"Those idiots. Where were they when I needed them? Did they ask for me then? Did they wonder where I was then, huh? Let's stay here. It's good for me here."

"Rudy, please, we'll come back. I promise. Let's get settled. Tonight's a big night. Zoya made reservations at a new restaurant. They have gypsy music. And the hotel has a sauna!"

"A sauna. Do you really think that will bring me back to life?"

I got up and turned away so he couldn't see my face.

"Of course it will, guaranteed."

Zoya took the luggage back to the hotel in a taxi without us. Rudy wanted to walk.

"It's cold out there," I warned him.

"It's good. It's my country."

I was still warm from the hot bean soup Valentina served us. She spread the black bread thick with butter. "I have to admit, the trip is worth making just for the bread."

"Yes, but did I ever tell you the story about the beans?"

"Yes, please I know. Beans in the camp. That's what they fed you. Let's leave before the sun goes down."

Rudy wore someone's overcoat and Alex's scarf and fur hat. My heart swelled as he lifted his smiling face up to the sun. He looked twice his size.

"Hi up there," I called out.

"Ahh, Chernovtsy."

People looked at us and smiled. They knew Americans, like they always did. Rudy whistled that Volga song as we walked briskly through the snow.

"It's wonderful, isn't it?" He looked down and squeezed my arm. After a few blocks, he pointed to a street off to the side of the boulevard. He raised his eyebrows and tilted his head in a question.

"No, Rudy it's too cold."

"Look, I promise. We will take a taxi the rest of the way. I just want to see my house. Please, just for a minute?"

We walked and slipped down Ivan Beguna. One minute he held me up. The next minute I held him. We were laughing so hard we had to stop to catch our breath.

"Sort of like our life together," he said.

His remark caught me off guard. "What?"

"I said holding each other up is the way our life has been, don't you agree?"

"Yes, you could say that."

"Surprised huh? Didn't expect me to admit it, did you?"

"Well, I just didn't expect you to see it that way. I thought you thought you held me up all the time."

"You really fell for that? You think I don't know the truth? I know. Even that." Rudy paused to check out my face. "It's like the gypsies say, it's us against the world."

We took two steps and both slipped and fell. "You did that on purpose, you bastard."

"At least I made you laugh."

"Have I told you lately?"

Rudy looked delighted with himself. "That you love me?"

"Yes."

"And I suppose you want to make something out of it?"

"Yes, as a matter of fact I do."

"Go ahead, make something out of it."

We sat in the middle of the street on the ice, oversized, over-stuffed children. I stuck out my cheek. Rudy kissed it, switched to the other one and kissed that too.

"You crazy Americans," he said.

CHAPTER 30

The swing hung on one rope in the empty courtyard. "You asked for it," I said quickly when I saw his face.

"Yes, it's okay. It's winter. What would I expect? Look there are footprints. The gate is open. Somebody is here."

I knocked at the door. No one answered. Rudy knocked harder. Unbelievably, old Boris came to the door. Boris had been married to Regina's sister. He was bent over and wore at least two sweaters and a scarf wrapped around his neck and up to his chin. The sun was in his eyes when he looked at us. I understood the equivalent of "who's there?"

"It is me, Boris. Rudichka."

"Rudichka? Rudichka!" Boris threw up his arms. "Gizella, Gizella," he called back into the apartment. As the men hugged and rocked, an old woman appeared out of the darkness behind Boris. She too was bundled in what looked like everything she owned. Boris introduced Gizella, his new wife.

Rudy added in English, with a wink, "She is not really his

wife. You know how things are here. Convenience. It is all about convenience."

"Not only here, you know. Do you think he may marry her on his deathbed too?"

"Cute."

Boris and Gizella ushered us into the house like we were royalty. The same oilcloth covered the table in Regina's old kitchen. The rags hung on their nails. An electric cord lay across the top of the tiny, unplugged refrigerator. I watched Rudy's eyes settle on the yellowish cloth that covered the empty jars on the windowsill, the ones that once held Regina's pickled tomatoes. He made a strange groaning sound.

"Are you all right?"

"Yes," he said in a choked voice.

Gizella apologized for not asking us to take off our coats or being able to make us tea. "There is no electric right now," she explained, "but it will be back soon." She shrugged her shoulders as though it has been turned off temporarily for some unknown reason. I heard Beno's name. Rudy sat with his head down. Boris patted his shoulder.

"What is he saying?"

"He is telling me about Beno's last days before we got here. He kept asking for me. Boris is trying to make it sound like it wasn't too bad. He is also saying that life these days isn't too bad either. He's lying obviously. Look around you. I'll bet there's no food in the refrigerator."

"It's not plugged in."

"Well, there."

While the men and Gizella talked, I walked around the apartment. I could almost hear the tinny Yiddish music that night of Rudy's birthday party. I saw him dancing with the old women, Regina lifting her shoulders, dancing on young girl's feet with her Rudichka.

The closed shutters in the back room only allowed slits of light to fall on the narrow bed we had slept on. Regina's embroidered initials were there on the pillow covers. A burned down candle on a low table was next to the bedpost where Rudy hung his pants.

Rudy's hopeful voice was behind me. "They want to know if we will sleep here tonight."

"Are you crazy?" I turned and saw him standing in the doorway with Boris on one side and Gizella on the other. They looked as though they were walking him down an aisle to meet his bride. I hesitated. There was that stillness around us, the one that reminded me of the other times. "Do you know what the temperature is in this house, in this room?"

"I told them we will think about it."

"Right. Tell them we will think about it. Tell them that we will get into trouble if we don't sleep in the hotel, remember?"

"You know I could work around that."

"Don't even try."

Back in the hotel room, Rudy kept muttering that some things never change, while I dialed the desk downstairs. I handed him the phone. He said a few words and slammed down the receiver.

"What happened? What did she say?"

"What did she say? What do you think she said?"

"She said it's closed."

"Right you are. The sauna is closed. Why? Because it is."

Rudy tossed his outer clothes on the floor. He threw himself on the bed. "There goes your last chance to bring me back to life."

"It's okay, go ahead, rest. We have plenty of time till dinner." I covered him, pulled off his shoes, and tucked the ends of the blanket tight under his feet.

I sat by the window and watched the people down in the street turn into shadows moving against the snow. Then I sat on my bed and watched Rudy sleep. Once more I studied his thin mouth, the deep wrinkles around his eyes, his hair against the pillow. Rudichka they called him, a boy, a pet. I laid down in the narrow space next to him and slid under his cover. A minute later there was a knock at the door. Rudy didn't stir.

The chamber maid in the hallway was bent with the weight of two steaming pails of water. She stared at the floor. I stepped aside. Without a sound she set them down in the bathroom and left. My watch said I'd been asleep for an hour.

I washed the best I could and went to wake him. There was an instant when he didn't move. Then he took my hand, kissed it and sat up.

"Guess what I've got for you," I teased.

"A drink."

"No, dearest love. Hot water. In a clean pail."

"How lucky can I get? Can I expect soap too?"

"Yes, look." I held out the little piece of soap.

"You must be kidding."

"For a guy who complains every time he washes his hands in New York, you're getting awfully particular."

"Next you will be reminding me gypsies can be dirty on the outside because they are clean on the inside."

"Come to think of it . . ."

Rudy slammed the bathroom door. I banged on the door, pretending to be angry. "Open up. Open up I say."

He opened it a crack and revealed one eye. "Yes?"

"Never mind."

Zoya waited for us in the lobby. She wore a bright red dress and fresh makeup. She apologized about the sauna. Rudy glanced at her fleetingly with his most impassive face, said no problem and changed the subject to getting a taxi. He was cold sober. Knowing he needed a drink made me so uneasy I wondered if I wasn't better off when he'd had a few drinks.

Rudy jumped out of the taxi. "Can you believe this shit?" he said in English. His cousins, the neighbors, even Boris and Gizella waited in the cold outside the restaurant.

"What's the matter?"

"They won't let them in."

"How do you know that?"

Rudy didn't answer. I followed as he ran down the steps to the subterranean restaurant. The manager and waiters jumped to rigid attention when Rudy burst into the lobby. In response to his loud demand they proceeded to scurry around, taking his coat first and then the others.

"Zoya, what did he say?" I asked.

"I can't repeat it. Please. But it certainly worked, didn't it?" The gleam in her eye made me both proud and jealous.

"Yes, it certainly did."

One couple occupied a table in the corner. There were no other guests. Three musicians, one playing the accordion, one the cimbalom and one the violin were grouped around a pale teenager. His morose gaze was fixed on the floor as he fingered the bass resting on his shoulder.

Rudy snapped his fingers for the waiter.

"Don't you think it would be nice, just this once, to ask people what they want?" I suggested.

"Don't worry about it. They want everything." Rudy gestured to his people around the table. "Look who we are dealing with. I will order everything on the menu. And a little vodka too."

"A little?"

Rudy laughed. "Well, maybe a little more than a little."

I ignored Rudy's joke. "The music is kind of dry, don't you

think? I wonder what happened to the kid Zoya raved about. The one playing the bass looks like they just dragged him in from the street. Look, he doesn't even blink."

"Give him time. It takes time for the gypsy to warm up, and money too."

Straw baskets of dark bread and dishes of pickled cucumbers, cabbage and tomatoes appeared with great ceremony. The champanski in the ice buckets all tilted toward Rudy.

"You ordered Champagne, not vokda? I'm impressed."

"No, I didn't. It's a gift from the owner because of the shitty way he treated my guests."

We all stood to toast. "Na Zdorovie," we shouted in unison.

"See what a little money will do?" Rudy shouted in English.

"I thought it's because they love you, remember?"

"That too." He raised his glass to toast to their health in return.

Rudy walked to the gypsy playing the violin. He spoke to him for a second, patted him on the shoulder and returned to our table. "It won't be long now."

He raised his hands and clapped over his head as the music suddenly picked up a vibrant beat. Everyone joined in. Even the kid on the bass suddenly had color in his face.

Rudy gulped down a third glass of champagne. "Will you dance with me?"

"I wouldn't miss it for the world."

"You are not being sarcastic are you?"

"No, dear. It's just if I don't get this dance in, it might be too late." I was hoping he'd question me but he didn't.

Rudy unbuttoned his jacket and stretched out his arms. The blue initials on his shirt cuff peeked out. "I am not going to drink that much tonight."

"Oh, really," I said. "What's the occasion?"

Rudy slipped his arm around my waist. He took my hand and rested it on his shoulder as though I didn't know how to do it myself. "Maybe I have had enough." He looked over my head and nodded to the gypsies.

"Just like that?"

"Just like that what?"

"Just like that, after all my years of nagging and carrying on?"

Rudy shrugged. "I guess I am like my King."

"That was about marriage, not drinking."

Rudy looked down at me. "Yes, that too."

"What are you saying?"

"I'm saying let us see what the night brings." The guests murmured behind us when he spun me around.

The musicians retreated to their table during the break. They smiled and refused the bottle Rudy sent over. The waitresses brought out platters of steaming food that seemed to glow from the champagne. I closed my eyes and listened to the tinkle of glasses, the clattering dishes, the animated conversation. Rudy's leg was tight against mine under the table. I leaned back in my seat and held up my glass for more champagne.

"Watch it, Schveetheart," he scolded.

"Maybe it's my turn."

The music started again. I looked up to only three musicians this time. The one with the violin was gone. Now the boy was the one who held the violin, and with a face so alive that for a second I thought he was someone else. I tried to say something to Zoya but she couldn't hear me. She smiled, nodded and gestured that he was the boy she told me about.

The boy's stiff white shirt stood out from his long thin body. His wore black boots and pants that were baggy at the leg but hugged his hips. His cheeks were smooth. With his chin resting on the violin, he rolled his eyes up toward the ceiling in concentration as he played. For a second his brow wrinkled as he looked down and around the room, turning his body as if to check out his audience.

I bent over toward Rudy. "What do you think?"

"He's got it, all right." There were tears on Rudy's cheeks.

"I've never heard anything like it. Are you happy?"

"Of course I'm happy. Can't you see I am happy?"

"Yes, I can see." I reached across the table to cover his hand with mine.

The music, the violin, the boy were one. As his bow moved up and down, his fingers played across the strings and his body swayed. The haunting melody was strange yet familiar. I let go of Rudy's hand and hugged myself to stop the chills.

"Can't take it, huh, kid?" Rudy put his jacket around me.

"It's beautiful. No human can make music like this."

"Right. This is not just another gypsy boy."

I looked around the table. The eating had stopped. Rudy's glass was still full. Everyone appeared to be under the boy's spell. One melody blended into another as the food got cold.

The boy bowed his head to our clapping and cheering. The color in his face, his posture all seemed to change as he gently laid the violin back in its case.

I motioned to Zoya to meet me in the lobby.

"Who is that boy?"

"You like his music, no?"

"Oh, Zoya, there is such a powerful longing in his music. Rudy talked about this yearning, this longing for years. I must meet him."

"Just like that?" The edge was back in Zoya's voice. "Do you think it is easy to know a tzigone?" Zoya stopped the manager and asked him a question. He looked at her with a blank expression and shrugged.

I caught his arm as he walked away. "Zoya. Ask him to call

the boy out here." Zoya asked him. He shrugged again and went back into the dining room.

"Zoya, have you ever heard playing like that?"

"No, it is true. He is extraordinary. That is a good word, no?" Zoya placed her hand over her heart and sighed. "The music, it has such, fatalism."

"Yes."

The boy followed the manager to where we stood. His eyes were fixed on the floor.

Zoya told him that I, an American, wanted to meet him. His eyes met mine for a split second before he looked down at my extended hand. He didn't take it. Zoya asked him something. He shook his head. "He does not understand Ukrainian, or Russian."

"How can that be?" I asked.

"It is possible." She asked him if he spoke German, Romanian. He shook his head no. He glanced up at me again, swallowed and said, "Polski."

"What, what was that? Polish?"

"Yes, Polish," answered Zoya. "I do not speak Polish. Nobody here speaks Polish."

"Oh, yes, they do. Wait." I crossed the dance floor. Rudy was in the middle of a story. He was reluctant to get up until I told him there was a gypsy waiting for him in the lobby.

"Rudy, ask him his name."

"His name is Pioteck."

"Pioteck? That doesn't sound like a gypsy name. Come on Rudy, cooperate."

"He comes from Poland. It's a Polish name. He's visiting relatives here. He says if you like you can call him Peter. He says that will be his American name, for when he comes to America someday."

"Tell him I prefer Pioteck."

Rudy used the word gadje in his next question. The boy looked at me. They both laughed.

"What did you tell him? I heard that word, gadje."

"Well, well. Don't tell me you are trying to learn their language too. Don't bother. Even I only know a few words. Remember, I told you they don't want us to know. In any case, you are gadje, you know. It only means that you are not tzigone, not a gypsy. That's all."

"Like you are? If I'm gadje, what are you?" The boy looked back and forth from me to Rudy with an amused look on his face.

"Ask him where he learned to play like that."

"I can't ask him a dumb question like that. This boy was born with a violin in his hand. Okay, I will ask him but I will tell him it is your question." Rudy put his hand over his eyes in mock embarrassment.

The boy's answer took a long time. "He says he learned from his grandfather and his father. He says that his father was the one playing the violin first tonight. He wants to know if we really think he is good. This is the first month he has played in public. He is seventeen years old."

"Tell him he is the best in the world. Tell him how we've traveled all over, and that's how we know."

Pioteck's smile widened as Rudy told him what I said. He grabbed Rudy's hand and shook it vigorously.

"He wants to know if you think they will like him in America."

"Don't tell him Rudy. Just tell him we are Americans and we like him. Change the subject. Ask him where his father went."

"He says his father will be back soon. He went to help someone who has a problem in the family."

I remembered the gypsy girl I'd seen earlier, the baby in the sling on her back, the freezing temperature. "Ask him if we can help."

Rudy hit himself in the forehead. "I don't believe you. Look outside. Do you know where these people live? They are probably dying from the cold out there. And, Miss America, you do not help gypsies. They do not want your help."

"Ask him anyhow."

"I will not."

"Rudy, you'd better ask him."

"And if I don't?"

"I will take matters into my own hands."

"What does that mean? You can't even talk to him."

"I know where he lives. Zoya told me. You go over that river of yours. They live right there, under the bridge."

"Would you do that?" Rudy looked at the boy. He looked back at me.

I held my wrist up to the light. Pioteck's eyes opened wide. He backed up two steps.

"Now look how you've confused the boy." Rudy put his thumb over my wrist and nonchalantly lowered my hand.

"You do remember, don't you?" I asked.

"Yes, of course I remember." Rudy mumbled something to the boy who then bowed.

"What's up?" I asked.

"Patience." Rudy took my hand and led me up the steps that went to the street. "Let's check the weather."

It was snowing again. The few people on the street bent against the wind that pulled the door from Rudy's hand. "This is wonderful, look it's a blizzard." He stepped out into the snow to grab hold of the door.

"Do you really think so? Our visa is running out."

Rudy brushed the snow off his arm. He turned and placed both my hands on his chest.

"Mmm, romantic, and sober too," I crooned.

"We could stay here you know."

"Sleep in the restaurant? I don't think so."

"That's not what I mean."

"What do you mean?"

"I mean, stay here, in Chernovtsy."

"Like for how long? Another week? Do you think they would extend our visas for another week?"

"Not just another week." In the dim light Rudy's calm face had only a few fine lines. "I mean stay here. Forever."

"Forever?"

"I belong here." Rudy talked faster. "You know that. You always knew that. You are doing okay here too. I know it is cold but I will keep you warm until the spring comes. I promise. I kept you warm that night in the bunker, remember, when you came from City Island to find me? I can do it again. We won't eat much. You said the bread alone is worth everything."

I was too amazed to say anything.

"We can do it. I need to stay here. Stay with me. You could write, about my people, the gypsies, this new country."

"And Olga Kobylianska?"

"Who? Oh, yes Olga Kobylianska. How do you know about her?"

"You know who she is?"

"Of course. I learned about her before they took us out of school. By the third class everyone knows our hero, how do you call it?"

"Heroine."

"Yes, that is what she was. Who told you about her? Zoya?"

"Yes."

"She picked quite a person to tell you about. There are so many stories about Kobylianska. You cannot imagine everything she did. How I wish you could read her stories. I cannot read Ukrainian but if we stay here someone can read to you. I will hire someone to come every day to translate, page by page. I will arrange it. For you.

"I can make her famous."

"You see. It's a wonderful idea. You know I was a boy when they took us to the Chernatu station to send us to the camps, but I remember . . ."

A blast of icy wind interrupted Rudy's sentence as the door opened. A man with icicles hanging from his mustache stumbled in, almost falling on top of us.

Rudy grabbed him and the man said spaciba, and straightened up. Rudy switched to Polish as he dusted off the snow from Pioteck's father's jacket. Then they walked down the steps together.

"Rudy?" I called to his back, but he didn't hear me. I turned and saw the snow, the rushing people, Chernovtsy through my reflection in the glass door.

CHAPTER 31

Rudy was about to make a toast at the gypsies' table. There was a pile of American bills next to an empty champagne bottle. Pioteck's music filled the room with longing.

"Rudy, I don't feel well." I lied. "It's time to leave."

"You must be kidding. We just got here."

"We have been here for hours. I want to go."

"I cannot leave now. Look, they love me."

"They love your money."

"Again?" Rudy slammed his hand on the table. "Do you have to say that? Do you have to hurt me like that?"

"Take it easy. Shhhh, quiet. Your voice is too loud. Look at you, your face is all red."

"Let's get this straight, once and for all. They love me. Do you hear? They love me. They all love me." He dropped into a seat and rested his head in his hands. "They. Love. Me."

I felt the sobs inside him when I touched his shoulder. "Look, I'm sorry. I didn't mean it."

He didn't move.

"I said I'm sorry. You hear me? I'm sorry."

"They are all sorry. Remember? Gypsy tears. All of them."

"But I really am."

Rudy looked up. "And where have I heard that before?"

I couldn't think of anything more to say.

He turned his back to me. He started to sing one of his sad camp songs in Yiddish to the gypsies.

The manager left to find me and Zoya a taxi. He was back in twenty minutes with no taxi.

"Zoya, what should we do? What would you do if I weren't here. How would you get home?"

"I would take the streetcar. It runs all night."

"There's a blizzard out there."

"We are used to such things. It is no problem."

"That's what we'll do then. Take a streetcar."

"Are you sure? It does come every few minutes."

I looked back into the dining room where Rudy danced with Valentina. His head was thrown back as he spun her around and around. I waved goodbye to the others. They were still eating, drinking, and singing and clapping.

The Retro was a block from the streetcar stop. I hung onto Zoya's arm as the wind whipped my coat around my legs. The snow was coming right at us.

"You know, Zoya . . ."

"What? What did you say?"

"You know, Zoya," I shouted, "sometimes only another woman can help."

Zoya's fur hat was low down on her forehead. The scarf up high over her nose muffled her answer. I saw only the slits of her eyes.

She pulled me to the center of the tight group of people

waiting for the streetcar. Soft, padded bodies pressed against
me, moving me toward the approaching streetcar that stopped
with a screech a minute later. I felt warm breath on my face, on
the back of my neck.

I heard Rudy's words. We could stay here.

The dismal hotel room was suddenly an old friend. I was
filled with gratitude when I heard the hissing that came from
the radiator. A few minutes later a girl delivered two pails of
hot water. I thought smugly of Rudy as I used all of it. I took
my time, rubbing extra lotion on my cheeks that were now
rough from the wind. I slipped on one of Rudy's clean, starched
shirts just for spite.

I propped myself up on all the pillows and tilted the lamp-
shade for more light. I drew a timeline on my pad, putting
March 21, 1942 in the middle. The names with dates next to
them came next, Rudy's mother Eva, my mother, my father,
my grandmother Bessie. I saved Beno, Regina, and Olga for
last. I wrote gypsy girl, baby, and added the Bronx, Chernovtsy,
Poland, City Island, Sadagura, Shady Nook, Mountain Lodge.
Soothing classical music filled the room when I turned on the
radio. The pad and pen dropped to my lap as I drifted into a
dream filled with clouds of snow.

A loud knock broke through my sleep. "Who is it?"

"It's me."

"Rudy? You must be kidding." I jumped out of bed. The cold
floor sent an icy jolt through my bare feet. The heat was off
again. "Is it really you?"

"Yes, of course, open the door."

I turned the lock and dashed back to the bed.

His frame filled the doorway. Icicles hung from his ears and
nose.

"I thought you said it was you."

"It is me."

"No, it's not you. It's Dr. Zhivago. No, it's the abominable snow monster."

"Stop laughing and help me. Can't you see I need some help here."

"Oh, you need help? He needs me," I sang. "He needs me."

"Okay, I'm sorry. I should have come home with you. Is that what you want to hear? Now will you help me get these clothes off?"

"Who helped me when I came home?" I asked.

"But I walked."

"Don't you dare take another step. Just stand there and take it all off."

Rudy worked silently. He peered into the bathroom. "The pails are empty."

"Your water would be cold now anyhow."

"That's true." Rudy walked to my bed and pushed himself under my cover.

"My God, you're like ice."

He squeezed his frozen feet between my legs to warm them. "It's just for a second, please."

"You promised to keep me warm, remember?"

"That was only if you promised to stay," he laughed.

"Oh." I squeezed my legs together. "How's that?"

"Wonderful. By the way, I believe you."

"You believe me what?"

"That you are sorry."

"It's about time."

Rudy moved closer. He lifted my face and kissed me on each eyelid.

"Mmmm."

"We could live like this," he whispered.

"We do. I'm falling asleep."

"Good. Remind me to tell you about Pioteck's father in the morning."

"What about him?"

Rudy's voice came from far away. "He is the king."

"The king, mmmm, that's nice."

"Not my King."

"Good. I'm tired of your King."

CHAPTER 32

I woke on my side with Rudy up tight against me. Bright sunlight fell on my outstretched arm. Children's laughter rose up from the street. I wanted to check the clock but dared not move away from the warmth under our cover. I remembered my dream. The gypsy girl was there, with her blue baby, on a throne in the middle of a snow-covered field. The jewels in her crown, not diamonds, but jewels of ice caught the sun.

Rudy's arm was thrown over my hips. His breath was warm on my back when he said in a sleepy voice, "Stay here."

I tried to slide out slowly. Rudy reacted immediately, tightening his hold and kissing my shoulder. "Good morning, Schveetheart."

I turned around and slipped my arm under his neck so he could rest his head on my breast. "Are you all right?"

"No. I don't think so."

"No? You never say no." I tried, unsuccessfully to sound

calm. "What's the matter?" Was he yellowish or was it my imagination?

"The pain is back. I am not even moving and it is back. And my arm is asleep."

"It's time for a doctor. Enough is enough. We're supposed to leave tonight at midnight."

"Let me think about it."

"You have exactly three minutes while I get dressed. And don't move out of that bed."

The girl with the hot water knocked on the door.

"They must listen at the door until they hear our voices. Ask her, Rudy. Ask her about a doctor."

"What does she know. She's a peasant. Look at her."

"Ask her anyhow."

Rudy hesitated. I knew he was about to say something he had never said before. Part of me was hoping he wouldn't say it. If he did, it would mean he was in really bad shape.

He talked to the girl. I heard the word medicamente. He pointed to his chest. The girl nodded and backed out of the room.

"What did she say?"

"She says there is a doctor nearby."

A minute later the phone rang. "Zoya says the chambermaid told her you need a doctor. She will be right up with one."

I sat on the opposite bed looking down at my trembling hands. "You were lying on your arm all night. Maybe that's the problem. Maybe you have a pinched nerve from the way we were sleeping."

"You think so?" Rudy bit his lower lip. "But we always sleep like that."

I used my most reassuring voice. "It'll be all right, you'll see."

"Aren't you going to say anything about my drinking last night? You're acting almost nice to me."

"What's the use? Rudy?"

"Yes?"

"Rudy, what were you going to tell me last night when we were falling asleep?"

"Pioteck's father is a gypsy leader. They are here from Poland to visit relatives. He said I could bring you today."

"Whose idea was that, yours or his?"

"Actually, it was mine." Rudy groaned as he moved to his other side.

"Can I get you something? A glass of water?"

"How about a drink? Yes, all right, water."

The old doctor in a baggy suit carried a cracked leather bag like American doctors used in the old days. He did not acknowledge me but walked quickly to Rudy and took his pulse. Zoya just nodded to me while the doctor rubbed a stethoscope on his pants to warm it. His brow wrinkled as he listened to Rudy's heart. He looked back at me for a second before he checked Rudy's eyes. Rudy moaned when the doctor lifted the cover and pressed down on his side. It was when the doctor said something to Zoya that I realized he was not aware Rudy spoke the language, and Rudy's blank face said he was not about to let on. For some reason Zoya didn't either.

"What did he say?" I asked.

"Nothing much." Rudy's calm voice infuriated me.

"What's the sense of lying? Zoya will tell me anyhow."

"Then ask her."

"Zoya, what did he say?"

Zoya looked down at the dresser and touched Rudy's tie. "He says Rudy has had one drink too many."

"That's not a diagnosis," I said.

"It is in this country." Zoya said something to the doctor. He turned toward me so Rudy could not see and tapped his own chest, over his heart.

"What was that he did?" Rudy lifted himself on his elbow. "I heard him say it was my liver. What did he just do?"

"He motioned that it's your heart, not your liver," I answered.

"But he said liver, I heard him."

Zoya interrupted. "It is both."

"What?" Rudy's raised eyebrows belied his calm voice.

"He said both," she repeated. "He said liver and heart."

"Oh, great." Rudy fell back into the pillow. He threw his arm over his eyes. "It is just a hangover. Tell the doctor it is just a hangover."

"Don't tell him, Zoya."

Zoya looked from me to Rudy and back to me again. She was silent.

"Okay." Rudy talked to the doctor. The doctor laughed. Even Zoya smiled.

"Zoya, now what did he say?"

"He told the doctor he has an appointment with a king, that he had better fix him up with some medicine real fast."

"Cute. You know, Rudy, you're very funny."

The doctor opened the side pocket of his leather bag. He produced two bottles of pills. He told Rudy to open his mouth and he put a tiny pill under Rudy's tongue.

"Is that nitroglycerine?"

"Yes, and the others are for his liver. He must take one every three hours."

The doctor sat at the end of Rudy's bed and looked at his watch. We waited silently.

Suddenly Rudy bolted up and slammed his feet to the floor.

"Ah, that's better." His face was no longer pale. "Who says these people are backward? Look at me. They know what to do. A miracle. My pain is gone."

The doctor poured the tiny pills into an envelope and made a long speech. Rudy looked up at him with unusual respect.

"What did he say?"

"He said I should only take these if I have pain."

Zoya cleared her throat.

"Oh, he said I should take it easy and when I get back to the States maybe I should see a doctor."

Zoya cleared her throat again.

Rudy glared at her.

"He said these pills will only keep him going for a short time. He must get help. He said that drinking is out. There are no miracle pills for the liver. He must stop drinking."

Rudy reached out to me and waved his hand in mock annoyance. "Will you please hand me my pants?"

"No, wait." I touched the doctor's arm. "Zoya, don't we have to pay him? What do we owe him?" The doctor shook his head.

"Nothing, the hotel takes care of it."

"Are you sure? Look how he shakes his head. Are you sure it's not because he feels sorry for Rudy?"

"Yes, I mean no."

At the door, the doctor turned and said "do svidaniya" with a terrible sadness in his eyes. I wondered how many people like Rudy he sees in his country.

"Thank you, Zoya." Rudy's deep voice was sincere. "And by the way, we will be all right today. You can take the day off."

"Are you sure? It is my job you know."

"I know, but we have a date with the king. I think it has to be just the two of us. We will be fine." Rudy winked at me. "Just fine."

On the way down for breakfast Rudy said something that made the elevator man slap him on the back. He waved gaily to the girls behind the front desk, and made the waitress blush.

We were alone in the dining room. "You look beautiful this morning." Rudy covered my hand with his on the white linen cloth. "It is a good day today."

"It depends on how you look at it."

"How do you look at it, gypsy girl?" He bent over and touched my earrings. "Have I seen these?"

"No. Do you like them? I've never had the nerve to wear them before."

"Why? They suit you."

"Do you really think so? I wore them for you."

"For me? Don't ever do anything for me." Rudy's face was alive with his most radiant smile. "And your skirt's long enough."

"What?"

"Your skirt. Let me see, stand up."

"Here." I stood up, twirled around and sat down quickly.

"Good, good. A decent gypsy covers her knees. So, you wore the earrings for me. Don't do that."

"Liar. You love when I do things for you. Remember? We hold each other up."

"Yes, but yesterday we both ended up on our asses."

"That was yesterday. Today is different. You just said so yourself. Today is a good day."

The waitress served the same breakfast as the day before.

"You had better eat," Rudy said. "You have a big day ahead of you."

"I can't bear it. Oh, the salami. I can't. Maybe a piece of roll." I sipped the tepid coffee and watched Rudy finish his own breakfast and then mine. "So how is it we don't need Zoya today?"

"It's just like I said. The king invited us over."

"You mean Pioteck's father?"

"Yes." Rudy wiped egg yolk from the corner of his mouth.

The snow hit the window behind him. "It's cold out there."

"Haven't you noticed? It is always cold here." Rudy rested his chin in his hand like he was talking to a child. "It always snows here too. Doesn't stop a gypsy though, does it?"

"No, I guess not. Wait a minute. What about you? The doctor said you have to take it easy until we leave. You aren't actually thinking of going to some gypsy camp today?" I crossed my arms over my chest and tightened my lips. "I refuse to let you go."

"Cute, you look cute. Enough with the dramatics. Today is a very important day. It is our last day in Chernovtsy. And I'm going to do what I need to do. And you are coming with me."

"And if I don't?"

"You will. Believe me. You will." Rudy slid his hand back to the middle of the table and turned it over. "See? Clean, no grease, no machine oil. Hold my hand."

I took his hand and held it tight against my cheek.

"Remember you threatened me?" Rudy said. "You told me if I didn't help you would go there yourself. Remember? You bragged that you knew just where they lived."

"Yes, but I had had all that champanski."

"You're making my hand wet, Schveetheart."

"Rudy?"

"Yes?"

"Rudy, you're not going to die are you?"

"Not today." Rudy threw his head back. His laughter echoed through the empty dining room. "No, I didn't plan on it today."

"Be serious. For God's sake, be serious."

"I am serious."

"You promise?"

"That I won't die today?"

"Yes, that you won't die today."

Rudy slapped his forehead. "I don't believe this woman. I will not die today. Okay? Are you happy now?"

"No."

"Good. Lets go up and get dressed for outside."

CHAPTER 33

We were on the bridge that linked Chernovtsy with Sadagura when Rudy told the driver to stop.

"Rudy, here?" I asked. "Can't we at least go to the other side, maybe into the little town first?"

"This is the place." His voice was so serious I didn't dare say another word.

People with shoulders hunched against the wind walked across the bridge in both directions. With the sun gone it was now a damp, cold morning. The edges of the river were iced, but under us the dark water swirled.

Rudy leaned over the railing and looked down. I pressed against him. "The River Prut, where it all began, and where it all ends."

"Ends?" I asked. "What ends?"

"Once we crossed this river it was all over. It was the end. Believe me, you can never go back. Even after we were liberated it was still all over. Oh, your body went back, you survived.

You put one foot in front of the other and walked back across this bridge. But you, the real you, never went back." Rudy stuck out his finger and pointed his hand toward the water. I waited for him to press the imaginary trigger. Instead he dropped his hand and sighed. "The way I see it, there was just too much shit under the bridge."

"Seems like you had a little fun by this river too, if I remember correctly." I forced a laugh. "Did you forget that part?"

"And that, Schveetheart, is why we are here." Rudy turned and touched my earrings. "Oh, just for the record, it was over there, in the woods."

On the Sadagura side of the bridge we stepped off the road and followed a deep path made by footsteps through the snow. The smell of burning wood permeated the air.

"Wait, stop, let me catch my breath," I said.

Rudy leaned against a tree and lit a cigarette.

"Why are you looking at me like that?"

"Are you cold?" he asked.

"No, as a matter of fact I'm not. I guess it's all the walking."

"Good, then take off the hat."

"But it keeps the heat in."

"Take it off anyhow." Rudy reached out and pulled on the hat. My hair fell to my shoulders. "Now you see, that's much better." He fluffed out my hair and pushed it behind my ears. "Much better. Now lead the way."

"What?"

"You, go first. Just follow the path."

"What's the difference?"

"Just do it."

I walked along the path with Rudy following behind me. We came to a ledge and looked down into a clearing and there they were, the gypsies of Sadagura.

A fire burned bright red and yellow in the center of the camp. Campers and shacks back under the trees had their own fires as well. Cows were tethered to the trees and chickens wandered around them. The horses were gathered together in a rough sort of corral.

"Rudy, look!"

He laughed. "I know, I know. I promised you, didn't I? Welcome home."

"Home? You silly thing."

"Ashamed are you? Don't be. With me you never have to be ashamed." His eyes sparkled. "Besides, it is no shame to be a gypsy. A little cold maybe, a little poor maybe, but no shame."

I pushed him hard and he let himself fall back into the snow. "On your ass again, Rudy?"

Rudy caught my foot and I fell, too.

"I don't believe we're doing this."

"Believe it. How many times have I told you?" Rudy strutted into the camp with his chest out, his head high. His open coat flapped in the wind.

"You look like you own this place." I said.

"Ah, yes."

Screaming children stopped chasing the chickens and geese when they saw us. Three women were arguing and wagging their fingers at a girl holding a baby.

"Look Rudy, it's the gypsy girl I saw in Valentina's building."

Rudy glanced at me for a second with his eyebrows raised but didn't say anything. Two men who were smoking and drinking from steaming cups nodded as though they were expecting us. They motioned for us to take their seats at the makeshift table by the fire while they went to find someone. Faint violin music came from one of the campers.

"Rudy, am I dreaming? I mean, this can't be happening."

Rudy smiled and didn't say anything.

I looked around at the colorful clothes stretched on the bushes. "Do they really think clothes will dry in this weather?"

"Eventually they will. These people have patience, they will wait till spring if they have to. At least, you see they do wash their clothes."

"I can see that." A woman looked up at us over her tin wash tub. Next to her, steam rose from the water in a black iron kettle.

Pioteck's father came out of his shack. Rudy greeted him and called him Baro Shero.

"What was that?" I asked.

"Baro Shero, it means he is the big shot."

Baro Shero wore the same clothes from the previous night. He slapped Rudy on the back, called out to the other men and gestured us to follow him.

We were ushered to a worn couch in a shack that was neat and clean. A delightful warmth emanated from the small fire in the center. Its smoke curled through an opening in the top. The men filed in behind us, took seats on the wooden chairs, or squatted in the corners.

Pioteck's round mother exposed her three remaining teeth when she smiled at me. She slid a carpet under my feet, touched my earrings and nodded approvingly. Then she set out a tray with cups of real, hot coffee, and proudly dropped cubes of sugar into my cup.

The children and women came in last. They scrutinized us before lining up against the walls. A chicken sneaked in. Everyone laughed while it pecked at Rudy's shoe. The gypsy girl was the last to enter, with Pioteck at her side. She carried the baby, he, the violin. I saw instantly, from the light in her eyes that she remembered me. The couple came up to us like we were royalty, bowed slightly and stepped back. The baby was crying. The girl put a scarf over herself before taking out her breast. Rudy's cheeks were flushed. He looked away.

Suddenly everyone seemed to be talking. "There is so much chattering going on," I shouted to Rudy. "We are quite a spectacle, aren't we?"

"Yes, of course. How many gadji do you think come here? None. They don't like strangers anyhow. So it works out fine."

"I guess it's thanks to you we are here then."

"Yes, as a matter of fact, it is."

"Brag, brag. You know, this is not exactly your ideal tourist spot."

"It is winter. Gypsies don't handle winter well. You know a gypsy will give you ten winters for one summer. Are you comfortable?"

"What?"

"Comfortable, are you comfortable?"

"After all these years, you ask me if I'm comfortable. Do you realize you've never asked me that before?"

"Well, there is a first time for everything. Like being here for example."

"It's not the first time you've been here. You told me the story yourself. Do you think I'd forget?"

"Well, in that case it is not the first time for you either. Remember Grandma Bessie?"

I looked down and couldn't say anything.

"Remember her smile in that picture at Mountain Lodge?" Rudy put his arm around me. The fire danced in his eyes.

"What are they waiting for? Are they waiting for us to do something?"

Pioteck's father squatted down next to Rudy. I realized that while I couldn't communicate with anyone here, Rudy could only talk to Pioteck, his father, and his mother, because only they spoke Polish. The rest spoke Romani, which Rudy couldn't speak, except for those few words he was so proud of.

Rudy and Pioteck's father seemed to have reached an agreement. The father stood up, as did Rudy, and they shook hands for all to see.

"What's going on? What are you talking about?" I pulled on Rudy's sleeve. He sat down again. "Did you sell me to the gypsies?" I asked.

Rudy laughed but didn't answer. Pioteck's mother produced a bottle of wine that was obviously homemade. Her husband popped the cork, took a drink and passed it to Rudy. Without hesitation, Rudy threw back his head, took a gulp and passed it to me. "Don't chicken out now, gypsy girl, they are all watching you." Rudy was whispering through his wide grin as if they could understand. "And don't wipe the top either."

I took a mouth full but held the bottle so lightly against my lips a trickle of wine ran down my chin and onto my blouse. I passed the bottle on to Pioteck's mother.

Rudy blotted the red stain with his handkerchief. "This is a very important thing that is happening here."

"What? Spreading germs?"

"No. A gypsy never eats or drinks from a gadje's mouth. A white man is considered magerdi, unclean. Only the gypsy is pure, on the inside, you know."

"Yes, I know. You told me how many times?"

"Purity is on the inside, the outside doesn't count."

"So how come they are drinking from our mouths?"

Rudy cleared his throat to speak just as Pioteck raised his violin to his chin. There was a hush. "He is playing for you. I asked for a private performance. Listen."

Pioteck's music was haunting and sensual. After a few moments, his wife handed the baby to a woman nearby and walked to the center of the room. She took off her coat and kicked off her shiny black shoes.

"Rudy. I can't believe you would ask them for this. It's the middle of the day."

"I told you it would be a good day. Besides, I can't wait, we can't wait. We leave tonight, remember?"

Pioteck's body swayed to his music as the girl danced.

They didn't look at each other but it was obvious they didn't have to. Their movements fit together perfectly. I felt the heat rise up inside me.

"It's been a while, hasn't it?" Rudy squeezed my hand.

"Yes, it has. I thought you forgot me." I couldn't stop watching the girl's twisting body.

"No. I will never forget you." Rudy wasn't watching the girl. He was looking down at me. He stood up and pulled me up with him. He took off my coat and threw it on the couch along with his own. He put his arms around me. I rested my head on his chest and let the music work its way into my soul. His voice was muffled, and his face buried in my hair when he repeated, "I will not forget you."

The music stopped. The girl was back with her baby. Pioteck bowed in our direction. Baro Shero stood before us with his hands raised high above our heads. It was silent except for the clucking of the chicken and the contented baby sounds.

Baro Shero chanted in Romani.

"What's he saying?" I asked.

"I don't know. Hopefully it is what I paid him to say."

"You paid him? For what?"

"To make us members of his family, brother and sister, of Romipen."

He grabbed my hand and Rudy's and held them up for all to see.

"Rudy, you told him about my wrist?

"It was the only way. I told him about mine too."

"What do you mean, the only way? Wasn't paying him enough?"

"It was not enough to make us brother and sister. It was only enough to get us married."

The people closed in to make a tight circle around us. The Baro Shero lowered our hands, crossed at the wrists. He placed his hand over ours, closed his eyes and chanted, with his people joining in, and then with Pioteck's violin. The chant quickened to a lively tune. Suddenly everyone was moving, dancing, clapping their hands and shouting into the air.

The king let go of our hands and backed away to join in the dance. We seemed to be forgotten.

"Well, they certainly got a reason to celebrate in the bargain. Just what they love, you know." Rudy had our coats over his arm. He pulled me toward the door. "Now let's get out of here."

CHAPTER 34

We walked quickly into Sadagura without speaking. We sat on a bench in front of a post office and pretended to watch the people and chickens coming and going.

I had never seen Rudy so excited. "We did it," he repeated over and over. He lit one cigarette after another. "I don't believe it. We did it."

"You did it," I reminded him. "And you must believe it, you always say believe everything. You engineered the whole thing. You got us married by the king of the gypsies. Nobody will believe it in America. Nobody."

It seemed Rudy couldn't stop looking at me.

"Making up for lost time?"

"Maybe. You look so alive, so beautiful today. Stay here with me. Let us not go back to America. Please."

"Rudy, please don't do this to me. We must go back. Maybe another time. We'll plan things better. It's lovely here in

Sadagura. Next time we can stay longer. Right here in Sadagura. Look, even the chickens pick up their mail here. Come, let's look for a taxi. We'll talk more at the hotel."

Rudy pulled on my sleeve for a moment but then let go and came with me.

We couldn't find a taxi, and there were no longer any people walking either way as we started back across the bridge. Rudy stopped once to catch his breath and then again.

"It's a little spooky, don't you think?" I hugged his arm against me. "I mean this fog and the bridge and no people."

"Yes. It is like we are the last two people in the world, the last of the old-time lovers, remember?"

"Yes, Rudy, that's us. Are you all right?"

"You can never go back."

"But we did, didn't we? Look at us."

Rudy stopped for a third time in the middle of the bridge. He looked down into the water. He didn't say anything.

We were approaching the end of the bridge when his hand shot up to his chest. He leaned against the rail.

"Oh, God. I told you this wasn't the right thing to do. Now look."

"It's all right. Just give me those pills. I will be fine in a minute."

Miraculously a taxi started to come across the bridge. I raised my hand to signal it to stop. For a second it seemed the driver would pass us, but he must have seen Rudy, the way he was leaning on the railing, and he stopped short.

Rudy fell back into the seat and put a pill under his tongue. He called out to the driver, "Ivan Beguna." The driver made a last-minute sharp left turn and stopped two minutes later in front of the old gate. I jumped out and banged hard on the door so Boris would hear me. "Come, please help me with

Rudy, Rudichka." He did not understand me. He looked past me into the garden, looking for Rudichka. I took his hand and pulled him out to the street.

Rudy leaned heavily on Boris's arm. "It will be all right in a minute, just another minute," he kept repeating.

The pill took longer to work than it did at the hotel. We walked slowly to the back room where I pulled off his coat and helped Rudy into bed, our bed. I slid his shoes off and covered him up in Regina's white quilt.

"Ah," he sighed. "Home."

Gizella said the electric is on. She will make chai. I pulled up the little stool and sat by Rudy's side, warming his hand on my face. His eyes were closed but his breathing was lighter. Finally he opened his eyes. "It is okay. I'm okay again."

"Rudy?"

"Yes, Schveetheart." He caressed my cheek.

"You married me."

"Yes."

"But, what about your king?"

"Oh, that was just a story. I told you today would be a good day."

"You also said you weren't going to die."

"Right, I said I was not going to die today because today was a good day."

"That's not enough. You're scaring me."

"Don't be scared. Put some sugar in that chai, please." Rudy propped himself up and sipped the tea. "Look, I think the best thing now is for me to stay right here. I'll rest, I promise. Be a good girl. Get our suitcases from the hotel, bring them to Alex and Valentina's and tell them to bring them to the station tonight."

"Why? I can bring them back here myself."

"I know. But there is a lot of stuff, Beno and Regina's, that they want us to take. They need to put it together with our things in the big empty suitcases. That way no one will bother us at the border on the way back. When you finish at Valentina's, come back here. We will leave from here. The tickets for the train are in the black bag, in the zippered side pocket along with the passports. Check the time."

"You think you will be all right here? It's cold."

"It is fine. I love it. Remember the beautiful nights we had here? How Regina loved having us."

"Okay, I'll go. I'll take care of everything. Promise me you won't move from this bed. Promise me you will rest."

"I promise."

I stood up and kissed his forehead. He caught my hand and held it tight over his heart. "I love you."

"I love you, too, Rudy."

"Don't forget me."

"I won't forget you."

I stopped a taxi on the boulevard. "Hotel Cheremosh," I said.

I asked for Zoya at the hotel desk. They said she would be back shortly. In ten minutes everything was in the suitcases. I pulled open the window in time to see Zoya walking down the street below. "Zoya!" I shouted. She didn't hear me. "Zoya." I raised my voice and waved frantically until she looked up and waved back.

I took the passports and tickets out of the side pocket while I waited for her. I opened Rudy's passport and saw it was about to expire. I told myself to remind him to renew it as soon as we got back. My eyes filled with tears as I ran my thumb over his ten-year-old picture.

Zoya knocked and walked in. She saw what I was looking at. I sobbed and buried my head in her coat. Her hand rested on my shoulder. "Is he, is Rudy dead?"

"No, Zoya, he's not dead. But you should see him. He's so sick. He promised me though. He said he won't die."

"Oh." Zoya stepped back and handed me her handkerchief. "Well, I suppose that if he promised, it will be okay." At least there was no edge to her voice.

"Zoya, he's not like other people. Do you know what he arranged today?"

"Yes, a visit with a king."

"Zoya, it really was a king. The king of the gypsies who live by the river. He's the man who played the violin first at the Retro. The boy is his son."

"Did you have a nice visit?"

"Zoya, please don't sound so sarcastic."

"Tzigone, nobody has anything to do with them. They are liars, thieves. No wonder Rudy gave me the day off. What did you do? What did they take from you?"

"Zoya, listen." I pulled on her sleeve to make her sit on the opposite bed where she looked intently at her boots. "Zoya, the king of the gypsies married us today."

Zoya's head snapped up. She looked first into my eyes and then to the passport I held against my chest. "Just like that?"

"Just like that. Rudy made arrangements last night. It's like he probably planned it for a long time. This is a very big step for a man like him. He has this thing about his King. Do you know the story about that Romanian King? He was around when Rudy was a boy?"

"Yes, of course, everyone knows about him. He married his sweetheart right on his deathbed."

"Zoya, please help me. If I can just get him back to America, I know he'll be all right. We have the best doctors there."

"What do you want me to do?"

"First I need someone to take this stuff down. Then I need to bring it to Alex and Valentina's apartment. Rudy wants them to bring it to the station tonight. They need to repack it with Beno and Regina's things mixed in. He wants me to tell all the cousins and neighbors to come to the station. I think he's hoping they'll have a little farewell party for us."

"At the Chernatu station?"

"Yes, he would love that. Can you come with me now?"

"It's a problem at this moment. A group arrives from Moscow. I must be here to greet them. But do not worry. I will catch up with you later. Let's get some help."

The elevator man carried the luggage and lined the suitcases on the pavement in front of the hotel. It was snowing again. Zoya leaned on my shoulder to write a note to Valentina telling her of our plans, suggesting they have a farewell party for Rudy at the station. "I will tell them to be at the station at eleven tonight. That should give us enough time to have a little celebration, don't you think?"

"I suppose so. What time does the train leave for Bucharest?"

"What does it say on your ticket?"

I took the ticket out of my briefcase. "Twenty-three fifty. That's ten minutes before midnight right?"

"Yes." Zoya opened the door to the taxi and hugged me tight against her. "You crazy Americans." Tears streamed down her face.

CHAPTER 35

The driver carried the suitcases up to the apartment. I laughed to myself as I led him through the dark. Maybe Rudy was right. Maybe I did belong here.

Valentina wanted me to take off my coat. I shook my head and motioned I had to leave. I gave her the note. She showed it to Alex. They both nodded. I hugged them and led the driver back down the stairs.

The driver opened the door for me. Zoya told him to take me back to Ivan Beguna after this stop. I bent to get in, but then stopped and straightened up.

He spread his hands in a questioning motion. I motioned I wanted to walk. The driver looked up at the overcast sky and shrugged. He took only one of the bills I held out and drove away.

I tightened the scarf around my neck and pulled my hat down as far as it would go. I turned the corner. There was light coming from Olga's cottage. I walked to the back and stepped into the hallway. I looked up at the statue of Olga, at the intelligent, disciplined face, the mouth curved into the hint of a smile.

The sleeping ticket woman looked up with heavy lids, saw me and dropped her head back to her chest. The office door was slightly ajar. It was dark inside except for the flickering of Vladimir's candle next to Olga's picture.

I reached for the candle. Olga's eyes held that same hint of a smile.

Shadows of the huge snowflakes falling outside played on the far wall, bringing Olga's study to life.

Just one more look around, I whispered. I walked up to the glass cabinet over Olga's desk and checked behind me as I lifted the lid. I slid my hand gently over the bottle, the books with her precious writing, the pen.

The floor in the hallway creaked. I looked back at the doorway as I moved my hand toward the blue velvet. It was only my imagination. Maybe the old woman had shifted her weight.

As though it had a mind of its own, my fist closed around a small hard object. I bent over and lowered the candle. My fist was on the strip of blue velvet next to the watch and the bracelet. I took a deep breath and opened my hand.

Tiny fiery rubies encrusted a magnificent ring. I closed my eyes to make the room stop spinning. Was it here before and I hadn't seen it? Impossible. I wouldn't have missed such a thing.

I set the candle down and put on the ring. As I moved it around to catch the light, images from Olga's diary flashed through my mind. I saw her walking through the station, the people watching her, the boy watching her. I saw Rudy's people waiting. I saw the king, his hand over our crossed hands.

"I have no sons," Rudy cried out that day at Mountain Lodge. "I have no ring."

The ticket woman groaned. Her chair scraped the wooden floor. I dropped the ring in my coat pocket, closed the cabinet and picked up the candle. I stepped back and pretended to be looking at a painting.

She came into the room and called out something that sounded like "Who's there?" She reached out for the wall switch. The room filled with light. She saw me, smiled in recognition and wagged her finger. She made a speech, threw her hands up and slapped her thighs. She pointed to an imaginary watch on her wrist, motioned I had five more minutes and left.

I paced the floor. I dared not take the ring out. I never stole anything in my life. But how could I put it back? I must put it back. They'd know immediately it was me. Vladimir would know. I remembered him polishing the glass with his elbow after that German touched it. I walked to the window and looked up. Rudy needed the ring. I needed it for him. If I took it now, Vladimir wouldn't know until tomorrow. We'd be in Bucharest by eight in the morning. The plane would leave at ten. By the time he realized it was gone we'd be on our way back to America. If only I could explain it to him. Maybe he'd understand. Such a sensitive man, dedicating his whole life to this woman, Olga Kobylianska, whom he hadn't even met.

"Damn." I squeezed the ring in my coat.

It sprang open, like a locket! I turned my back toward the door and carefully lifted the ring, cradling it in my palm. The ruby-covered lid had indeed sprung open. And inside, there was a white diamond. Without a thought I snapped the ring shut and dropped it back in my pocket. When I got to the doorway, I turned back for one last look. The old woman was coming up behind me, mumbling in her language.

I followed her out to the hallway where I put Vladimir's candle at the base of the statue. The old woman rested her hand on Olga's knee and looked up at her. "Ah," she said and looked at me. "Ah, Olga Kobylianska." She placed her other hand over her heart.

I extended my hand and said goodbye. She took it, studied it for a second, then kissed it. "Do svidaniya," she said.

CHAPTER 36

I moved slowly and carefully up the slippery hill to Kobylianska Boulevard. It took all my strength not to run. The snow was piling up in drifts and there were no taxis on the boulevard, but it wasn't far. I'd done this walk with Rudy. My hand was in my pocket with the ring fitting perfectly in my fist. It was just the way Rudy had described it, and the way Regina had described it to me. Oh Rudy. I kept calling his name silently into the wind.

I stayed close to the buildings where there was just snow. Before I had Rudy to hold onto, now there was no one. My cheeks burned from the wind, my feet were numb. It didn't matter. I was almost there.

"Boris," I shouted, banging on the door with my one gloved hand. It took so long, but Boris finally opened the door and I fell into the kitchen.

"Rudy?" I searched Boris's face. "Rudichka?"

Boris smiled. He stretched out his hand out toward the back room. "Rudichka."

I took off my coat and quickly switched the ring to the pocket in my skirt. Gizella brought me the same old gray flannel slippers Regina used to give me. She spread my coat, scarf, and hat in front of the green tile oven. I realized it was warm at the same time I saw the small pile of wood in the corner. Boris pointed to himself to let me know he'd gathered the wood for this fire. I patted him on the arm and stood before it rubbing my hands together. Gizella gave me a tray with steaming chai and crackers to bring to Rudichka. There was a candle too, in a hurricane glass in case the electric went off again.

Rudy sat by the tall window in the big faded chair I knew had been Beno's. On the table in front of him lay an open album with sepia-tone pictures. He looked up over his reading glasses. "Schveetheart, you've come back to me."

"And where would I go on a night like this?"

He started to get up, but I pushed him back into the chair. "Stay there. You look so comfortable. Boris's bathrobe, is it?"

Rudy parted the lace curtain and put the album on the windowsill to make room for the tray. I sat in the chair opposite him and poured the tea. He took off his glasses. "You look beautiful tonight."

The light from the electric lamp on a high dresser behind him fell on his head. "You don't look too bad yourself. You know, the way that light is shining on your head, you, well, you don't look too bad yourself." The lines in Rudy's face had softened. His mouth was relaxed, not that tight thin line I was used to. "You look so relaxed."

"Would you believe they won't let me smoke?" Rudy whispered. "It has been four hours. Maybe it is time. Maybe this is a good time to stop."

"Oh Rudy, that would be wonderful. You said it would be a good day."

Rudy looked at me over the cup as he sipped his tea.

"Rudy, I have so much to tell you. You won't believe everything that has happened. Wait until you hear this."

Rudy stood up. He turned off the electric lamp and closed the door. He came back and pulled me up.

"It's a long story, but I know you love long stories." I said.

"I know."

"You know what?"

"Everything."

"There you go again. Please be serious. You can't know about this, about what I am going to tell you."

Rudy held my head against his chest, his fingers gently rubbed my scalp. "It has been a long time."

"Yes, it has."

"I've missed you." He lit the candle.

"But wait, what about my story?"

"This is more important."

I sank down into Regina's featherbed. Rudy's face was over me. The candlelight reflected in his eyes. I ran my finger along his ear and down to that soft spot. His warm mouth against my neck made me tremble. He unbuttoned my blouse. "You are right," I whispered.

"About what?"

"This is more important."

"Is that good?"

"Yes, yes, you said this would be a good day." I saw the snow coming down behind Regina's lace curtain.

"To make today really good, we have to finish it like this."

"Rudy?"

"Mmmm."

"Say you won't laugh. Promise you won't laugh."

He lifted his head. "I promise." His hand massaged the back of my neck.

"Tonight is different. It's, it's just different. Remember that night in Mountain Lodge, when we saw that deer outside the window?"

"Yes."

"Well it's the same here now, the same cold, clean air. Remember when I said it was the same cold, clean air as in Beno and Regina's house in Chernovtsy? Look, the moonlight comes in just like it did that night."

"And you stood in that moonlight and took your robe off. Remember that? And you stood there naked and took my hand. Like this, just like this."

"And we cried that night. You cried. That deer, remember how you said he was always running, tired of running."

"Say you need me."

"You said 'I can only survive if you need me,' remember?"

"They don't need me anymore." So tonight you are the only one."

"I do, I do need you."

"Then help me."

CHAPTER 37

I leaned over to check the time on my watch. We had been sleeping for two hours. It was almost ten o'clock. I listened for a squeak, shuffling slippers, anything, but the house was silent.

Rudy opened his eyes. "Shhh, don't worry. They are here."

"Who?"

"All of them."

Regina's lace curtain moved. The flame flickered from a draft of cold air that swept from the closed window across the room. I reached over to shield the candle. Rudy shifted his body lower under the featherbed as the cold wrapped around us. His arm was tight around me. He shuddered, pulling me down into his warmth. "Stay here with me." His serious voice reached down deep inside me. I snuggled up to him to give myself one more minute to feel him, to smell him.

"Rudichka, let's go." I tickled his feet with my toes.

"Don't do that. You know I can't take it."

"Can't take what, leaving or tickling?"

"Both."

"Guess what time it is. Guess."

"Eight o'clock. We have plenty of time."

"It's not eight o'clock. It's ten thirty-five."

"What?" I felt his body tense. "I don't believe it. Check your watch."

"I just did."

I jumped out of bed. Rudy sat up. "I don't believe it," he repeated. "What happened?"

"You know what happened. I hope you know what happened. And you'd better believe it, too. I believe everything." I stretched and giggled. "Come on, cowboy, git your pants on."

"I know everything and you believe everything. What a pair we are, what a pair."

"Did you know the Chernatu train station is over a hundred years old?"

"I know, you tell me every time we come here. And that before it was a train station it was a church. Rudy, I have to talk to you. All this rushing to the station, and before that, when can I tell you?"

"Soon, we will have plenty of time. Do you know gypsies still live in this station when it is very cold?"

"You told me that too."

A family was camped out in a grimy corner. The man was asleep on a bundle of clothes. The woman breast-fed a baby in her lap. A barefoot girl, perhaps three years old, approached us. She held out a dirty little hand.

"Oh she has no shoes, look."

"Haven't we had this conversation before? Rudy laughed. "She will get used to it. You can get used to anything. Remember that. If there is one thing I want you to remember, that is it." The girl held up her skirt, making a pocket for Rudy's change.

"Cleaned out, see?" He turned his pockets inside out for the child to see. "Cleaned out. Finally."

"Rudy, that's a lot of money you gave her. There are rubles there too." The child's eyes were alive with excitement.

"Shit money," he said. "Only shit money."

"What? I don't believe that. The money here is still worth something you know."

I expected to see the usual scorn on Rudy's face. Instead he looked down at me and smiled. "I guess you're right. I shouldn't talk like that."

"Mmmm, nice. How many years did that take?"

"I told you I am a funny guy. It takes me time. Besides, I have to be nice to you now."

"Why now?"

"Look, here they come."

Valentina, Alex, neighbors and other cousins bustled in from the side entrance of the station. They were covered with snow. I knew that meant they had walked. The next second Zoya and Vladimir rushed through the front door.

"Look Rudy, the lampposts in the street, they've turned them on," I said.

"You see. A farewell party. Perfect. And look, there's Boris and Gizella. I told them not to bother. Ah well, they love me."

Zoya carried a bunch of blue flowers wrapped in newspaper. "Rudichka, sit down, come." She led him to a bench. He pretended to brush off the seat and then gestured for me to sit down first. I shook my head in disbelief.

"Believe it," he said and laughed again.

"Zoya, what are they talking about?"

"They are commenting on how well you both look. You look different, radiant. And Rudy, looks, well, healthy. It is hard to picture that man in the hotel room."

"Yes, I think it is the air here," Rudy interrupted. He was

listening to both conversations at once. "I feel great. Why if there was a soccer ball around here I would show you how great I am. Zoya, did you know that I was once . . ." Rudy stopped talking in English in the middle of the sentence. I knew he wanted everyone to understand. I looked around at their eyes, all sparkling with admiration.

I stepped back a bit and watched as Rudy told his story, mostly with his hands. His hair fell onto his forehead the way I loved. They were gathered around him, his people. And they loved him.

Again I heard his words, "Stay here with me." I joked with him, laughed it off. Maybe I should have been more serious. This was where he belonged. This was where he was happy.

The loudspeaker interrupted. A hush fell over the station while they all listened to the nasal voice.

"What? I asked. "What did she say?"

"The Sophia-Moscow Express will be a few minutes late," Zoya answered.

"Oh, is that all?"

"Don't think it is some small thing," Rudy said in a suddenly serious voice. If the train comes a minute after midnight, they will charge us more money for the extra day."

Zoya handed me the flowers. "You will write to me, no?" She sniffed and blew her nose in her embroidered handkerchief.

I thought about the paper they don't have. "You know, Zoya, maybe when I get back to America and get settled again we could do some business, you and I. Your people need so many things. And the things you need are so common and plentiful in America."

Zoya looked at me in surprise. "That takes big money, like those Germans have. You don't have money like that, do you?"

"No, I don't. But I want to help. There must be a way. You know we have an expression in our country."

Zoya laughed. "Olga Kobylianska."

"What about her?" I held my breath.

"I was just thinking. You remind me of what she tried to do. Just one woman. We will never forget her."

"Well, I was going to say something related in a way. We have an expression in our country, something like, 'it is better by far to light just one candle then to curse the darkness.'"

"Oh, I like that."

"Maybe I can light one candle."

"Just don't forget us, no matter what happens." The loud-speaker blared again. "She's coming."

Rudy stood up and started walking toward the exit onto the platform. His people moved with him, each one carrying a suitcase. Zoya and I followed behind. It was snowing even harder, with wind that made it difficult to breathe.

Rudy grabbed my hand. "Look," he shouted over the wind. "Look, over there." He pointed to the end of the platform. "It's the king."

Sure enough there was Pioteck, his gypsy girl, the king and his wife. Rudy motioned to the others to wait, grabbed my hand and pulled me to where the gypsies were huddled under the lamppost.

The king said something to Rudy.

"What did he say?" I asked.

"He says they came to say goodbye because they did not see us leave the camp. They wish us luck on our journey, on our road. Now, what do you think of that?"

"I think that's great, considering they are not even allowed to be here."

Rudy reached out to the sling around the gypsy girl's neck when the baby cried. "The king says it is a girl."

"I don't believe they brought the baby here on a night like this.

"She has to get used to it, too."

Rudy continued his Polish conversation with the gypsies. They all looked very serious. I could tell something new had come up by the surprised look on Rudy's face. They came just to say goodbye, but now there was something else. The gypsy girl and I studied each others' faces while the others spoke. Then she reached into her coat and pulled out a silk scarf.

"She wants you to have it," said Rudy. "A gift."

"I can't take that. It's too extravagant, they are so poor. Look at the fringes, the colors. No, I just can't. Give her money, Rudy, offer her money for it. Then I'll take it."

Rudy told Pioteck. Pioteck repeated it to the girl. Her gold earrings made a jingling sound when she shook her head.

The train whistle echoed through the night air. The gypsies were backing into the shadow. The girl pushed the scarf into my hands. She said something to Pioteck who then shouted to Rudy over the wind and the screeching train.

Rudy translated, "She says take it for her daughter's dowry."

The gypsies disappeared into the dark as the train came to a halt.

"Rudy, what does she mean?"

"We will talk later."

People shouted and pushed to get on the train. Not everyone had a reserved sleeper like we had. The steam billowed up from under the sleeping car that stopped right in front of us. "I can't believe this craziness, this noise," I called back to Rudy.

"Believe it," he shouted back. "Believe everything."

I pushed my way through the crowd back to Zoya and the others. I was breathless when I pulled Zoya aside. "Zoya, there is no time to explain. Here. Take this. It belongs back in the cabinet in Olga's cottage." Zoya opened her mouth to speak. I put my finger over her lips. "Please, just do it, for me. Okay?"

Zoya nodded. She looked over my shoulder. "Where is Rudy?"

"What?" The bustling scene around me froze as I turned. "He's right here, behind me."

Zoya shouted out his name first. It was easy to see down the platform because almost everyone was on board.

"Rudy." I ran down the platform. "Rudy, what's wrong?"

"It's not too good," he gasped. He was hanging onto Beno's lamppost.

"Rudy, you promised. You promised."

His face was white. "The train was too late, Sveetheart, it's a new day."

CHAPTER 38

Mountain Lodge, New York, 1989

The sun is gone. I've been reading the depressing letter that came today from Ukraine. Zoya writes that winter is unusually brutal for November. They still have no fuel, no jobs, no recognition from other countries. I flick the switch for the lantern outside the cottage and hesitate to watch Rudy's fancy footwork with the soccer ball.

"Let's go, dear. Enough is enough."

He runs to the bottom of the stairs with the ball on his hip.

"Look how muddy your feet are. You can't come in like that."

He looks down at his bare feet and laughs.

"Rudichka, why do you refuse to wear those expensive soccer shoes I bought in the city? Look how cut up your feet are."

He lifts his head and smiles that smile he doesn't know he

has. "You have to stop calling me Rudichka, Mom. It's embarrassing. Jeffrey heard you in the school yard and told the other kids and now they're all making fun of me, calling me Rudichka, Rudichka."

"I'm trying. It's hard. You wouldn't understand, you're too young. And besides, it's a long story. Come now, walk on the newspapers to the bathroom. I filled the tub with hot water so you can wash your feet first."

"If I hurry, will there be time for a bedtime story."

"You didn't do your homework yet. And you have that big game tomorrow after school. You need sleep if you're going to grow up to be the world's greatest soccer player."

"That's the story I want to hear tonight. About how my father was supposed to be the world's greatest soccer player."

"We'll see if there is enough time. Let's get moving here."

Rudy hands me the muddy ball. "It feels like it's going flat. Ugh, what am I supposed to do with this? And I guess we'll have to go to the gas station in the morning before school. Get some air."

Rudy laughs and walks gingerly on the newspaper path to the bathroom. "At least it is not a schmataball."

"And what, young man is wrong with a schmataball?"

"Nothing mom. It's just hard to believe that he could have been so good, with just a schmataball."

"Well, believe it anyhow. If you want to grow up to be like him, you will have to believe everything."

About the Author

CORA SCHWARTZ is a photo journalist and behavioral psychologist who lives and writes in South Fallsburg, New York. Her essays and short stories have been published in journals and periodicals. Her most recent publication, *The Forgotten Few*, was written and photographed to fulfill a promise she made to her late husband, Rudy, which was to bring humanitarian aid to the remaining survivors in Mogelov. *The Forgotten Few* has been described as a small book with a huge impact. With only a few pages of text, the book presents photographs of holocaust survivors. They are images that will haunt the reader forever. *The Forgotten Few* is currently used in classrooms around the world.

Helping survivors continues to be Ms. Schwartz's mission as she visits Ukraine and supports organizations that deliver food and run soup kitchens there. *Gypsy Tears: Loving a Holocaust Survivor* is the personal story behind *The Forgotten Few*.

Ms. Schwartz also owns and operates a retreat in upstate New York for writers and others who need a place to stay and do creative work. This haven was founded in the spirit of a Ukrainian writer, Olga Kobylianska, who is considered one of the first feminists in Eastern Europe. Ms. Schwartz discovered the work of Olga Kobylianska on a trip with Rudy to his hometown, Chernivitsi. Since that time, Ms. Schwartz has communicated with scholars worldwide, taken courses on Ukrainian women writers at Harvard University, and published one of Olga Kobylianska's stories, "Nature." Ms. Schwartz's interest culminated in the recent delivery of a lecture at the Municipal Library of Chernivitsi, entitled "What Would Olga's Message Be for Today's Ukrainian Woman?"

Ms. Schwartz is currently working on the sequel to *Gypsy Tears*. She is expanding on Olga Kobylianska's philosophy, revolutionary at the time, that "we are all God's children, whites and gypsies alike." In an effort to authenticate this sequel, Ms. Schwartz is planning an extended stay in a cottage in Glinitsa, a suburb of Chernivitsi where some of the best Roma musicians reside in peace with their "white" neighbors.

ALSO BY CORA SCHWARTZ
The Forgotten Few

❧

For other titles from
Hobblebush Books,
please visit
WWW.HOBBLEBUSH.COM